SEMIRAMIDE   *Frontispiece*

TWO IN ITALY

BY

MAUD HOWE

AUTHOR OF "ROMA BEATA," ETC.

WITH ILLUSTRATIONS FROM DRAWINGS

BY

JOHN ELLIOTT

BOSTON

LITTLE, BROWN, AND COMPANY

1905

THE UNIVERSITY PRESS, CAMBRIDGE, U. S. A.

To J. E.

CONTENTS

ILLUSTRATIONS

I
ANACRAP'

TWO IN ITALY

CHAPTER I

ANACRAP"

I

FROM THE MARINA GRANDE TO "PARADISE"

THE boat that landed us at the Marina
Grande was rowed by an old gaffer
and a young boy. The fare, four
cents for each passenger, was accepted so politely that inevitably the tip which had not
been asked was added. On the quay a merry,
clamorous crowd of girls and women took possession of our belongings, a bandbox, a port-
manteau, a small Japanese straw telescope, a
guitar, Pan — the nightingale, from whom we
could not bring ourselves to separate — and the
sketching kit. All these had come with us
in the railroad carriage from Rome to Naples.
We have learned the wisdom of carrying many

small pieces and keeping them under our own eye. A tip of ten cents to the porter, twenty to the guard at the station — the thing is done, and the vexation and expense of having the luggage weighed and paid for is avoided. Our position in that island world was fixed by the women who handled our packages so deftly; then and there our places in the social scale were allotted.

"Semiramide! be careful with the instrument! Accidempoli! do you handle a guitar as you would a sack of potatoes? Excuse her, my Signors, this is not her work."

Semiramide, who had been trying to carry both bird-cage and guitar, relinquished Pan to the speaker, Olympia — a gray-haired beauty of fifty — and turned liquid, apologetic eyes upon us. I wondered what Semiramide's work was; she was a flower-faced child of fifteen, with teeth like new-peeled almonds, hair a sunburned thatch of straw color, with an under shade of new cast bronze.

"Where do their Excellencies wish to go?" Olympia demanded.

ANACRAP'

"To the Paradiso."

"To Anacrap'? We are of that country. When I saw the steamer's smoke I remembered there was fish to get for the master's supper. As long as we must come down to the Marina, why not help the strangers to land? But do not mention it to my master, he is such an original! There is a good cabman — he who squints — the carriage with the yellow wheels. He has a good horse, he will take you for two francs to the Paradiso."

"Do you expect to get into Paradise at so small a cost?" I asked. Olympia threw back her head, and, whether she understood the joke or not, laughed at it. Semiramide only stared at us timidly.

"She is your daughter?" I asked. The resemblance was strong.

"I cannot deny it, but she is afraid of her own shadow. The Sisters have had her since she was *so* high; it is time for her to come out into the world a little. She is not so stupid as you might think; she can use her needle like a nun."

5

TWO IN ITALY

When they had tucked us and our belongings safely into the cab and seen us started on our drive along the winding carriage-road which leads from the seashore to the upper plateau of the rocky islet, Semiramide, Olympia, and the other women took to the short cut, the way of the seven hundred steps, which from the time of Tiberius till the days of Victor Emanuel (when the new road was built) was the only path from the Marina Grande to Anacrap'. Our road made a wide loop and came back far above their heads. They looked up, laughing, at us, just as they looked and laughed at Burne-Jones when he caught the impression that remains for our joy in his "Golden Stair."

That drive was a spiral of delights; every turn of that corkscrew road gave us a finer and wider view of the sea and sky that the poets have sung from Theocritus to Verlaine — almost prepared us for the draught of beauty awaiting us in the garden of Paradise. The cab stopped suddenly; my view was obscured by the guitar on the box, beside the driver.

"What place is this?" I asked.

6

ANACRAP'

" Paradiso ! " The answer came from the
other side of the wall.

" You hear ? " said the driver, a man of few
words.

" Paradiso ! " The raucous cry was repeated
as we walked through a gate in the wall'to the
garden. At the back there was a long, shaded,
out-of-doors room, with only one side wall, —
that of the house. Under the centre arch hung
an immense blue and orange macaw swinging
in a hoop.

" Paradiso ! " It was the bird's greeting and
farewell to coming and departing guests.

The best rooms were all taken by a family of
opera singers—fortunately for us—those rooms
are sure to have been stuffy, with upholstered
furniture, carpets—pretentious and uninterest-
ing. With apologies and misgivings, Philippina
(a daughter of the house) led us up an outside
stair to an upper gallery hanging over the
garden, from which our rooms opened. Silent
rooms at the top of the house with nobody over
our heads, — bare, delicious rooms, with brick
pavements and furniture of iron, painted white.

7

TWO IN ITALY

Dinner was served in the garden; our table was an old marble slab resting on the capital of a Corinthian column from the Villa Jovis of Augustus.

"White or red?" asked Philippina, a flask of each in her hand. That is always a serious question; we knew the white wine of the district, which bears transportation and appears on the wine list of the Café di Roma; the red was an unknown quantity.

"Which do you advise?" Philippina smiled mysteriously, refusing to commit herself. "That all depends on the taste. Some Signori prefer one, some the other."

"Take the white; whatever else you drink, touch no water unless you wish to have typhoid," said a tall man sitting at the next table.

"So that is the serpent in this Paradise?"

"You have said it."

We had not noticed him till he had spoken — there was so much else to see! In front of us the glories of sea, sky, and distant shore; behind, the corridor hung with lobelia, splendid

8

ANACRAP'

bougainvillea, cape jessamine, and other rich
flowering plants I did not know. In the midst
the gorgeous macaw, restless in his hoop,
greeting each new comer with his shrill
" Paradiso ! "

After the spaghetti with chicken livers, the
"mixed fry" of artichokes, red mullets, and
cuttlefish, the braised beef and carrots, quails
and wild asparagus salad were served. Our
neighbor, who had been silent since his warning about the water, spoke sharply to Philippina.

"What! you offer quails to me? What
ails you, *figlia mia ?* Do you mistake me for
one of those accursed Germans ?"

He spoke with such heat that I suppose we
looked as much surprised as we felt.

"You are strangers, you have still to learn
the admirable habits of these islanders. They
spread huge birding nets across the mountain.
This island is the place where the quail, flying
north from Africa to the coast of Europe in
the spring, and flying south in the autumn,
alight to rest on their long flight. They have
9

yet to learn, poor things, that the island is more cruel than the sea; they fly into the nets and are caught by thousands, kept in cages, and fattened for the Roman market."

"As they were in the days of Lucullus?"

"Exactly. We ought to have gone a little farther by this time. To protect them, I bought that hill-top " — he pointed behind him — " but they get around it; they manage to place their accursed birding nets so that they still catch their victims without actually trespassing on my land. Savages!"

I had no stomach for my quail after this and pushed back my plate; this seemed to give him satisfaction.

"You are Americans — English?"

"Six of one and half a dozen of the other."

"Few tourists have the sense to come here at this season; perhaps you are not tourists?"

We turned the question.

"Well, trippers or residents, it does not matter to me. I have got one of your people up at my house; rather a remarkable man, not long for this world, though he does not know it ; something very queer with his heart. He seems to be without a friend in the world except Olympia and Semiramide. If you don't mind meeting your kind on this side of the water, you might come and see him."

"When shall we come?"

"To-morrow. Here is a card ; you must show that to the person who answers your ring or you'll not be let in."

"Will eleven o'clock suit you?"

"Perfectly. Philippina, give these people good coffee to-morrow morning. None of your chicory now — the kind you keep for me. Here, Odin! Come, Olaff!" He strolled out of the garden, — of which he seemed to feel himself master, — followed by a white wire-haired Russian wolf-hound and a heavy-eyed Great Dane.

"Paradiso!" screamed the macaw.

"Good-night, Polly," said the departing guest. When he was gone we looked at the card. It had no name, merely the pencilled words, "Admit the bearers."

OLYMPIA

II

WE rang the bell and waited in the hot street, face to face with the blank, whitewashed Oriental wall that might hide a palace, a prison, or a lazaretto. After the third ring, soft, padded footsteps were felt rather than heard; we knew that if the gate were opened it would be by one who wore the *soccie*. There was a faint creak made by the rusty hinge of an invisible wicket; we had the irritating sensation of being inspected from within. I have not the hearing of Henry the Fourth for nothing; I caught the whispered words, " Open, open, child, it is the strangers of the bird-cage."

The bolt was shot back, the gate opened, and Semiramide greeted us with curtseys and smiles.

" *Favorisca!* " (do me favor of entering).

Olympia stood on a ladder, picking grapes from the pergola which sheltered one end of

13

the garden. A little, hacking cough sounded close beside us. It came from the shadow of a large tree. We looked to see our compatriot, and found sitting on one of the lower branches of an umbrageous ilex a small gray monkey, holding under its arm a furry white rabbit which it seemed to be squeezing unmercifully. I stepped forward to interfere in the rabbit's behalf, when the stranger of last night came out of the house.

"Take care, Giulietta's teeth are sharp; she does n't like strangers, ladies in particular. Poor thing, her temper is worse than ever, since she took this last cold; she will not live long."

"Are Giulietta and the rabbit very friendly?" I asked.

"Giulietta, yes; not the rabbit. Giulietta suffers so with the cold, especially at night, that if it were not for the rabbit she would have died long ago. She uses the rabbit like a muff, and keeps herself warm by hugging it."

"The rabbit does not object?"

14

" I am afraid the rabbit does not like it very
much, — it is the fate of the inferior animal to
be sacrificed to the superior. Three rabbits
have died since Giulietta came. She does not
mean to hurt them, for she realizes how important they are to her comfort; the trouble
is, she holds them too tight; after a time, the
difficulty of drawing a long breath knocks
them out."

We asked for the American.

"He does not appear till luncheon, which is
at twelve. You will stay and take it with us.
Olympia has prepared for you."

The invitation — it was more like a com-
mand — had a compelling urgency. We did
not hesitate for a moment; we did not even
exchange a glance before accepting, for — I
have not told you — the garden and the house
were, on the whole, the best house and the
best garden I have ever seen, which, remembering my pilgrimages, is saying something.

Luncheon was served in a long, cool room,
with windows that looked out through the
pergola to the sea, so that between the white

15

columns and the bay hung great, purple clus-
ters of grapes and sun-browned vine-leaves.

As we entered, a large man with a bald head
as round as the dome of St. Peter's got up
from a seat by the window.

" Here are two of your own people, Incognito, come to have luncheon with us," was
the host's introduction.

" The best people in the world," said the
American, shaking hands with us; "they are
even worthy of Olympia's macaroni."

Olympia makes the best "*fettucie fatt' in
casa*" in the world; a fresh, home-made macaroni fit for gods, for epicures, and for us. The
service suited the place, Olympia from the
kitchen door directing Semiramide, whose
color came and went deliciously as she offered
each dish. The dishes and goblets were of
uncommon form and material; the vast, iri-
descent sea-shells heaped with oranges and
purple figs were admirable.

" Where is the mongoose?" said the American.

" The mongoose, like some others, dislikes

16

strangers. If you can all be perfectly quiet for five minutes, perhaps he will come in," said the host, putting a plate of food down on the floor behind his chair. We ate as silently as we could. Presently there was a little, hurried pitter-patter, a pause, then another, and by a series of short, timid runs, the mongoose sidled into the room and up to its plate. It ate daintily, like a cat, with furtive, upward glances at us. When it had finished, after nuzzling its sharp little nose for an instant in the hand the host held down to it, the mongoose slipped away, waving its pretty tail.

It was not till we were having coffee in the pergola that we really got a good look at the American; he had sat in the darkest corner of the dark room and inspected us, as if he did not wish us to see him too well. Once in the sunlight, the wine of the grape — or of good-fellowship — melted away all reserve. The talk was as good as the wine. If I could have bottled it and poured it out for you (as the vintage of those purple grapes hanging before our eyes was later poured out) I could make you a rare feast. Alas! It was of a quality both stimulating and evanescent. The American was a learned man — not a pedant. He carried his knowledge lightly; offered it to you as if it were a glass of whipped syllabub, always assuming that whatever he imparted was equally well known to you, — that he was merely reminding you of this or that line of poetry, fact of history, myth, tradition. The host was not far behind him; he seemed surprised at his own communicativeness, saying in an undertone to the American, —

"Incognito, I have not talked as I have talked to-day six times in my life."

Each of us seemed to have dropped his every-day mask of commonplace, and with it his prejudice, his curiosity; the first personal note was sounded when the American said to the host, —

"You have never told me what brought you to this island."

"You have never asked me. My yacht was wrecked here. I was forced to land. I have never found any attraction strong enough to

18

take me away. Since questions are in order, what brought you here ?" He looked at us.

"The sight of your island; as we sailed by on our way to Greece, we caught the blue outline against the sunrise sky. It drew us like a magnet. Finding the steamer stopped to leave the mails, we got off with them."

"Tell them," said the host, looking at the American, "why you came here." He spoke in English for the first time; we had been using the language of the country.

"For a variety of reasons; I was tired —"

"You said," interrupted the host, "that as the stag howls for cold water, so longed you for — for —" He hesitated.

"As pants the hart for water-brooks," the American gravely corrected. "I was in need of beauty, of silence. I turned back the pages of the memory book, a good many of them, thirty-five years of them, till I came to the picture of the island where I had once found those things —" He paused.

"That was before the new road was built ?"

"Before the road, before steamers, before

19

many things,—mere surface changes. I found, as I had left, the three things by which this people has ruled the world, — grace, charm, beauty. I left Olympia on the Marina Grande ; I found Semiramide."

"Tell them that — tell about the first time you saw that good creature ! "

"Olympia was offered to me as a human chattel. She was the age of Semiramide then. I had the money they asked for her in my pocket. I found that she was in love with a blackamoor who dived for coppers when the boats came in. I put the price they had asked for her into a *dote* for her, and saw her safely married to the Moor. He was an ugly fellow, but she liked him even more than I liked her, which was saying something, as she possessed the cardinal virtues — beauty and silence."

Olympia's voice broke the ensuing pause.

"What ? Head of a cabbage, you have not pulled off those vine-leaves as I told you ? You allow the grapes to remain half covered, when they need all the sun ? May you drink

nothing but sour wine all your life, you and
your miserable dead!" Olympia was scolding
the gardener's boy.

"I wish she possessed the gift of silence
now!" groaned the host.

"Could you find it better personified?"
Semiramide, who had brought in the liqueurs,
was speechlessly offering him the tray.

"Benedictine; yes, the large bottle. To
Chance!" The American lifted his glass.
"We owe her this meeting, we owe her every-
thing worth having in life!"

II

THE INN OF PARADISE

CHAPTER II

THE INN OF PARADISE

I

AT THE INN

THE opera singers had rehearsed "La Bohême" till after midnight. I fancy we shall never listen again to that sublime translation of Bohemia into music without thinking of the garden of Paradise, of ourselves sitting among the orange-trees, just where we could not see into the rooms whose windows and blinds were open. There had been a hot musical discussion at dinner. As they all talked *fortissimo*, none of it had escaped us. It was the prima donna's birthday. They had, however, consumed less food, less wine, fewer cigarettes than usual. They generally sang in the morning when we were out sketching; to-day there had been an excursion; the music that had been bottled up all day was bubbling in their throats. The soprano hummed snatches from her aria in the restaurant scene; her husband, a basso profundo, rumbled out shakes and flurries of Coline's song like deepest organ notes with the tremolo stop on. At last they got to work. Oh! I shall hear "La Bohême" sung by greater artists, perhaps, but it will never be the same. For weeks we had lived under the same roof with the singers — had bowed to them gravely, morning and evening. We had seen their seamy side; they had been sometimes cross, sometimes boisterous, always a little *grossolano*, — untranslatable phrase; our nearest equivalent would be Big Hominy. But familiarity had not bred contempt. We liked those singers, they were so serious at their work, so serious at their play, — liked them, though we never spoke to them nor they to us.

I stole down to the garden to get an orange, — it was too early to hope for coffee. Pearls of dew rolled from the glossy green leaves down my sleeves as I picked the golden fruit, cold with the chill of night. The new-opened blossoms, unearthly in their spotlessness, looked more artificial than real.

" Paradiso ! "

I turned to see who could be about at that hour — the macaw, a faithful sentinel, never sounded a false alarm. Coming down the outer stair was the biggest man I have ever seen out of a show — a man of what sculptors call heroic size, dressed in long, sweeping garments of gray, his face lost in a tangle of gray hair and beard. The beard, long and knotted, hung down on his breast; the hair, tousled from sleep, stood up over his forehead in two horns. The sun, just above the hill-top, struck full upon this astonishing person, who carried a large something (it might have been the Tables of the Law) under his left arm; his right hand held together his trailing robe. He was the Moses of Michael Angelo, made flesh and blood ! I never lost that first impression, even when I realized that the gray robe was a large dressing-gown ; the Tables of the Law, a gray crash towel and a mammoth sponge ; that

Moses was on his way to the bath conveniently situated on the ground floor of the inn.

Later, when we saw him dressed and in his right mind, he was still a striking figure. With age's ready garrulity, he made friends with us over a sketch of J.'s, discussing it in odd, old-fashioned terms long since out of date. He had loved and known something about pictures back in the days of the 1830 school. Of later art and its blague he was refreshingly ignorant. Where could he have lived never to have heard of Whistler or Sargent? In farthest Ind — an attic of New York — a lunatic asylum?

In the garden of Paradise time is not; days — weeks — slipped by uncounted; the summons to keep a rendezvous in Athens broke like a horrid rising bell on a rosy dream.

"To-morrow we go," said J.

"Then I 'm for St. Agnese, to sketch the pavement."

Sitting at work inside the church porch, I heard Olympia harrying her master's favorite donkey.

THE INN OF PARADISE

" Angk ! devil of an ass, I say ! "

Olympia had certainly overloaded the little
donkey; his tiny hoofs slipped helplessly on
the square blocks of lava stone with which the
steep street was paved. Besides the huge pan-
niers of grapes between which he disappeared,
a heavy sack of flour was laid on his poor back.
To make him go faster, Olympia twisted his
tail. The creature gave a piteous scream.
Before I could interfere came interference of
a weightier kind.

" Olympia ! " The voice was so terrific that
the peasant, under all her tan, turned visibly
pale. It was our host of the villa.

" Wretched woman ! Out of the foolish
kindness of my heart I purchased, because you
are growing old, this faithful friend to carry
the burdens that belong by rights on your
miserable back. How do you reward the ass
and me ? By abusing, by torturing, this admirable, this long-suffering, this dear donkey ! "
He was paler than Olympia ; the hand he laid
upon the donkey shook.

" Pardon me, my lord; the creature has an

evil, obstinate disposition. Besides, frankly, now, between ourselves, the animal is not a Christian."

"Perhaps not; I had, however, hoped that you were one."

Semiramide, large-eyed and silent, stood by listening.

"There is no use trying to teach a stupid old woman like you anything; but for the girl's sake, come with me."

The door of the church of St. Agnese stood open; he strode in, followed by the two women. I went on with my sketch.

"Look at this beautiful picture," he began. "You know what it represents; the garden of Paradise, where, but for a woman not half so bad as you yourself, we should all be living now. Here in this beautiful church, built to do honor to the holy Virgin, they have painted on these tiles pictures of all the beasts. They did not put them on the walls or on the ceiling, as is usual, knowing well the character of the people. They put them here on the pavement where you cannot avoid seeing them every time you kneel down to hear mass. There is the donkey, the animal you say is not a Christian ; he wears a cross on his back in memory of Mary, who once rode with her holy Child upon an ass. Behold, here is Giulietta; Odin, the mongoose; all the beasts of the field and the birds of the air painted by a devout artist hundreds of years ago to teach you hard-hearted men and women of Anacrap' to be kind to the animals ! "

He eagerly pointed out the different animals. Olympia, watching the anger fade from his face as he talked, feigned deep interest in the strange old pavement of painted majolica tiles which covers the whole floor of the church. It represents an enormous tree of life, the roots of which reach the door, the tips of the branches growing up to the altar. The larger animals — the cow, elephant, giraffe, and croco-dile — are placed in the lower part near the door ; the birds and monkeys in the upper branches near the altar.

" The name, sir, of this strange beast, the like of which I do not see in Anacrap'?" asked

Semiramide, pointing to the figure of a unicorn. The question, evidently to her a burning one, was the only word I ever heard her voluntarily speak.

"That animal, my child, I have never seen. It does not live in my country or in yours. The English make many pictures of it " — he caught sight of me — " ask that lady, she has been in England, she may herself have ridden a horned horse."

Fortunately, Semiramide's courage gave out; I was spared the question.

"You now may go," said the host. Girl, woman, and donkey vanished. "They are more savage than some naked heathen black I have known. Poor people! it is not their fault, they are so ignorant!"

"They are very interesting."

"Of course they are. Aristocrats, scholars, bourgeoisie — they are the same the world over. To get the real salt and savor of a race, go to the peasant. I live among them because on the whole their company is less irritating than any other. To-day " — he tugged at his blond beard, for a moment visibly embarrassed; the only time I ever saw him when he did not control the situation, was not lord of the island, master of all the company — "to-day is the national holiday of my country ; on this one day of all the year I go out to the highways and byways to find guests, persons with whom I can sit at meat — persons of breeding." He hesitated ; then, with a return of arrogance, "Come, with the gentleman, your companion, and bring your friend, he who looks like the Moses of Michael Angelo. I do not say to dine ; that implies things you will not find. If, however, you will be at the villa at dinner-time, you will find food, wine, tobacco, and welcome."

" We shall not fail you ; as to him you call our friend — "

" I don't care to know his name or nation. Am I curious ? Have I ever asked yours ? You may be Brown, you may be Smith, you may be Robinson, you may be from — Alaska — Australia — it is enough for me that you are Anglo-Saxons."

"Bah!" I interrupted, "you know us for what we are, as we know you. Names, nationalities, which it is your whimsey to ignore, are not the essentials" (it was the only way to take him). "This man, Moses, you may also understand. We do not. He spoke to us, as you did, at the Paradiso. He shall have your invitation; he will doubtless accept it."

He did accept.

II

STRANGE old man! He stood with us when for the last time we rang the bell-pull, — a rose-vine of cunningly wrought iron that hangs outside the villa gate. There were changes in the garden. The grapes had all been gathered. They stood in great wooden tubs bound with iron hoops, waiting for the white feet of the girls who tread the vintage. It was mid October, — mid vintage; the island was steeped in the blood of the grape from mountain-top to shore; the smell and color of it was everywhere, more intoxicating than the wine itself.

After dinner we adjourned to the garden as before. The host poured out a saucer of weak coffee, half cream with three lumps of sugar, and put it at the foot of the ilex-tree, saying half apologetically, "Giulietta has what she calls her coffee with us."

Moses was as much impressed with the villa as we had been on our first visit.

" This is the ideal place for a man to lie *perdu*, — for one who wishes to forget the world and be forgotten of it."

" I find it so," said the American. " This island is one of the gems of the earth. It is as beautiful in its way as this jewel, which in honor of your feast," he bowed to the host, " I take pleasure in showing you." He drew out of his pocket a piece of yellow silk from which he took a prism and held it in the light. The rainbow colors fell across his hand as he turned the crystal from side to side. We gazed with fascinated eyes at the morsel that splintered the sunlight into the primal colors.

" One of the seven perfect jewels. It has been under my roof all these weeks without my knowing it!" said the host.

" That is the finest stone you ever saw, madam," said the American; " an old Asiatic gem; none of your passionless, clear-as-window-glass, drop-of-water stones; the fires of the earth smoulder in its heart; its cutting is a lost art." He put it in my palm, where, for all its fire, it lay cool.

"I did not know a diamond could be so wonderful," I said.

"Our host has told you no other diamond is. I have seen larger stones. This is the perfect diamond, the treasure it took the earth centuries to produce."

At first Moses said nothing. He seemed magnetized by the stone; his eyes never left it. When he finally spoke it was in an indifferent tone.

"Oh, yes, a fine stone; but what diamond compares with a ruby?"

A single drop of pigeon blood burned on the finger of his right hand, — a long, thin hand, prehensile, subtle, — a hand to fear.

"What," said the American, "will become of this gem when I have finished with it? Unfortunately, I cannot take it with me."

"You have probably already learnt all that it can teach you," said Moses.

"Unfortunately?" queried the host; "fortunately, I should say, for your heirs."

TWO IN ITALY

" Heirs ?   The little I have will go to
Olympia and Semiramide.   The girl has, the
old woman had, beyond all persons I have
known, the supreme gifts, beauty and silence.
The inheritance will not be enough to spoil
their lives. To leave them this diamond would
be a crime.   Fancy the number of lives it has
blighted since it was dug from the mine."

" The crimes committed in its name since it
was freed from the matrix," said the host.

" Appalling !   It is a very old stone ; seas of
blood must have been shed for it."

" Take it," I said, putting the diamond into
the host's hand.

" What would you do with it if it were
yours ? " asked the American, looking at me.

" Wear it."

" And be murdered for it," he scoffed.
" What would you do with it ? " he looked at
the host.

" Sell it to a museum where all you col-
lectors could enjoy it ; sink the money in
artesian wells ; make this isle of the sea a gem
of as pure a water as your diamond itself."

THE INN OF PARADISE

"And you?" The American turned to Moses.

"I should analyze it in the hope of perfecting my discovery of making diamonds. It can be done, but at great, at prohibitory expense; the stones produced so far have been small and valueless. Perhaps the missing knowledge is buried in the heart of that incomparable gem."

The silence that followed, weighted by the inexpressible longing in his voice, grew intolerable. It was broken by the American's crying gayly, —

"A song, my host, a song of your people."

The host went to the piano — it stood in a cool marble music-room opening on the pergola — and sang, to a fantastic accompaniment, —

"Radabim bamboola, radabim bagatago, radabim bamboola, Baltherasco Schnego. Schnego! Schnego! Schnego!"

He shook his great head, his mane of hair bristled, his body swayed as he dashed out the chords of the accompaniment with a power, a witchery, impossible to withstand. The song had several verses. At the second we were all on our feet, gathered around him, repeating with him the refrain — half-way between a roar and a sneeze — " Schnego ! Schnego ! Schnego !"

" That was a great song," I said.

" The greatest in the world ; let's have it again." He sat down at the piano a second time.

Now, if you can discover the language of that song, you will know, perhaps, from what country our host hailed, more than we ever knew.

" Who has the diamond ? " It seemed to me that the words only were mine, not the impulse to pronounce them.

There was a moment of silence ; nobody spoke.

" Did I not give it to you ? " I said to the host.

" You did ; but what I have done with it is more than I can tell."

" It will turn up all right," said the American.

" We must find it now," the host insisted.

" It has slipped into the folds of your dress, perhaps, or it may have worked its way into the garments of one of us men. We must search each other," said Moses.

I had quite forgotten his existence. At the words we all turned and looked at him as if he had only at that moment joined us. I was frantically feeling in my pocket, my dress. The host, grown pale, was for turning everything in the room upside down.

"We have heard quite enough about the diamond," said the American. "I insist that nothing more be said or done about it just now. We shall probably find it; if not, my difficulty about disposing of it after my death is solved."

It was growing late. I never passed a more uncomfortable quarter of an hour. It was out of the question to go until the diamond was found. J. and our host were undeniably restless. I was dumb with nervousness; only Moses and Incognito seemed perfectly unmoved. They talked and they talked, about everything on earth, in the sea, and under the earth. What had been to me a fountain of living inspiration became mere words, words, words! Incognito saw my trouble.

"If you friends are still bent on leaving by the early boat to-morrow, we must not keep you up too late. A parting glass to our next meeting, eh, Prince of Hosts?"

The host clapped his hands. Olympia brought in a tray with delicate Venetian glasses and a big *fiascone* of island wine. The host lifted the *fiascone;* the American gently pushed him aside.

"Let me fill the glasses," he said. He was rather slow about it, I thought. His back was turned towards the company: was it my fancy, or did a few grains of white powder fall from his hand into the first glass he filled? Finally he faced us exclaiming, —

"To your health, friends. Ah! it is a great wine. Clarence was right. He is not the first or last of the race drowned in wine."

He offered the tray first to Moses, laying a hand upon his shoulder to call his attention.

"This is your glass," pointing to the first glass he had poured out.

"No more wine; I have already exceeded —"

THE INN OF PARADISE

The hand laid so lightly on the shoulder grew heavy.

" You cannot refuse to drink to our departing guests."

For a quarter of a second Moses looked him in the eye ; then he glanced at the host, stroking the big wolfhound Olaff; at J., alert and tense ; at Olympia, sitting in the shadow halfway between the pergola and the gate, feeding Odin. Then he gave a little shrug of the shoulders, made a polite bow, looked at me, " *à votre santé*, Madame," raised the glass, and drank the wine at a draught.

I have never been able to recall the anecdote with which the host next entertained us. It was very long, doubtless it was interesting. I could only think about that diamond — how could we go till it was found ? — and watch the others. At a point in the story Incognito disagreed with the narrator. J. took a hand, and the scrimmage of talk grew hot. Moses and I seemed to be left out of it. The old man looked pale and weary, worse than weary, positively ill. The shadows began to deepen under his cavernous eyes, the sweat suddenly stood out upon his great forehead in drops ; from pale he turned green.

"The gentleman is suffering," I whispered. He rose from his chair and staggered to a sofa.

"Go now," said the American, "and go quickly."

I took my salts to Moses, made his pillow comfortable, and said, "What can I do for you?"

"Go!"

"Olympia will take you to the Paradiso," said J. "I must remain with our friend—" The American whispered something in his ear. Then I was bundled out of the room ; at the gate J. joined me.

"What did the American say to you?" I asked.

"If he had wished you to know, would he have whispered it?" said J.

"Oh, the diamond, the diamond!" I cried. "How can you leave till it is found?"

"I think he will recover the jewel," said J., coolly. That was all I could get out of him.

THE INN OF PARADISE

When we reached the Marina Grande the next morning, we found Moses on the quay before us, waiting for the steamer. The old man looked pale. I asked how he had got over the sudden attack which had forced him to spend the night at the villa.

" It was nothing," he said, " a mere touch of the sun."

A hail sounded from behind; the host and the American were coming down the way of the seven hundred steps to see us off; Olympia and Semiramide followed, bearing flagons.

While the host talked with us, my dreadful ears, which have heard so much that was not meant for them, caught a word here and there of what Moses and Incognito were saying.

" Why did you suspect me ? " asked Moses.

" You were the only person present I could suspect."

" Bear no malice," said Moses.

" None in the world, my dear fellow. If you will forgive that Borgia trick we will call it quits."

45

" How did you ever think of it ? "

" Man ! How do you suppose I ever got that diamond myself ? "

" The old story, eh ? "

" Well, you know how it is yourself."

The steamer whistled — once, twice — authoritatively. Olympia took the guitar, Semiramide followed with Pan ; we hurried down to the small boat of our friend the gaffer.

" You carry the essence of music with you in that wicker bird-cage, as I carry the rainbow in my pocket," said the American.

" You have the diamond safe ? "

"As safe as such a thing ever is. The night brought counsel. I would not soil the hand of any living woman by laying in it the finest diamond in the world. In a church of Rome is a beautiful marble woman. When you hear of a peerless gem set on the peerless brow of our Lady of San Agostino, you will know that I have looked my last upon the sun."

" *A bordo, a bordo, Signori !* " cried the old gaffer. We packed ourselves into his boat ; Moses got into another.

THE INN OF PARADISE

" A *fiascone* of wine and some figs from the
villa for your breakfast," said the host. A big,
straw-covered flask and a flat woven basket
were put in each boat. The gaffer cast off,
the boy bent to the oars, the boat shot out
from the shore. We got ourselves and our
many packages (there were some new ones, a
pile of sketches, and some antiquarian finds)
on board the steamer first; then Moses came
heavily up the gangway.

" Signore," said the petty officer who helped
the old man on deck, " have you not forgotten
something ? I see a basket, a *fiascone.*"

" Let them go," said Moses; " I have had
enough of the island wine ! "

We watched the white walls of the villa till
they blurred into the white clouds of the bluest
sky in the world. At the angle of the walls,
where the sandstone sphinx from Egypt looks
seaward, a flag was suddenly run up. The
host was giving us a parting salute. Our
glasses were packed ; at that distance we could
not see to what nation the flag belonged.

47

III
BUONA FORTUNA

CHAPTER III

BUONA FORTUNA

I

THE VILLINO

THE only answer to our ring was a furious barking of many dogs.

"Not up yet," said Patsy. "What lazy people!"

"*Chi è la?*" (who is there) came from the other side of the heavy door in the villa wall.

"*Amici!*" cried Patsy. "Is that you, Signorina? Are we too early?"

"No, no; only have patience while I call my brother to shut up the dogs. Attilio! Attilio!"

"I am not afraid of dogs," I said.

"You must be afraid of these dogs," Patsy insisted. "The poor brutes are kept savage purposely. Nobody is allowed to make friends with them; they are chained up all day like

wild beasts, fed on raw meat, and let out at
night to roam the garden and protect the
house; this is supposed to make them better
watch dogs. Only Vittoria or Attilio dares
go near them when they are loose."

After a deal of whining, barking, and
rattling of chains, the door swung open and
Vittoria welcomed us to the garden.

" Be not afraid of Bimba; since the Signorino 'mended' her little one's leg she attacks
none who come with him." A bullet-headed
brown and white puppy slept on Vittoria's arm;
Bimba, a lean pointer bitch, fawned on Patsy.

" Bimba's actually licking my hand; the first
time we met she sprang at my throat. Have
you had coffee yet?"

" I was just preparing it, — if you would not
mind having it out of doors?"

The garden lies between the house and the
studio. The breakfast-table was laid under an
arbor of Maréchal Neil roses. The grounds
— small for a Roman villa — are shut in by a
high white wall. The house is in the Moorish
style, with minarets and Alhambra tiles; we

52

seemed to be no longer in Italy, but in Granada.

"You still have that bad habit of taking milk in your coffee?" asked Attilio. "Milk is indigestible; we have none in the house. Vittoria will prepare your coffee with a raw egg beaten up in it. You will like the taste quite as well as milk; besides, it is far better for the stomach."

I remember the taste of that cup of coffee still, — it was nectar; to be sure, it was brewed by a goddess, that may have had something to do with it. Vittoria's profile is like the young Tiberius on the gold coin of my Roman fibula.

"Where is Don Manuel?" asked Patsy.

"In the studio, of course; been hard at work since daylight; must not be disturbed to-day; it's an anniversary!" Attilio nodded towards the house. Every shutter was closed; the only sign of life was the glimmer of the lamp on the altar of the chapel, where the casement was ajar. "It is the anniversary of his father's death, — a day of mourning, as you see."

"How long since Don Manuel's father died?"

"More than twenty years." Attilio sighed. "Between ourselves, brother-in-law carries these matters of sentiment a little too far. Fancy! the house will be shut up like a tomb all day; not a window may be opened. Then we must all hear a long requiem mass. Religion is a good thing, but—with respect *è un po' troppo!*"

"It is unfortunate," murmured Vittoria, "Gemma has to hear so many extra masses!" (Gemma, Don Manuel's wife, is sister to Vittoria and Attilio.) "When our mother of blessed memory died, Gemma made a vow that she would never again *sit* in church; she always stands or kneels. I persuaded her to sleep late this morning, to be fresh for the requiem."

"This was an unfortunate day for us to come—" I began. They overwhelmed me with assurances that it was not so.

"Will you have nectarines or apricots?" asked Vittoria; "both are ripe." On the other side of the marble fountain with the gold fish, not ten feet from where we sat, were two trees laden with fruit.

" Both for me, then," said Patsy, " and one of those lemons. Did you ever see such a fine one ? "

A ring at the gate was followed by a loud double knock. " That's Roberto ; he's early," said Attilio.

" Roberto," Patsy explained, " is a cousin, — a good fellow, though he is a priest."

" It would be as well, my friend," Attilio whispered to Patsy, " not to speak about the matter of the wine before Roberto."

" Then we'll be off," said Patsy. " I came to ask you about sending a cask to New York."

" Impossible ! It would ruin that wine to fortify it."

" I 'll not have it fortified. I will take the risk of its crossing the ocean."

" The ocean, perhaps, not the equator ; it would be spoiled by the time it reached New York."

" Why should it cross the equator ? "

" How can you send a cask of wine from Naples to New York without its crossing the equator ? By way of the north pole ? No, *figlio mio*, it is not possible; besides, I have none to spare; that's why you're not to mention it before Roberto. He is inquisitive, and he knows a good wine (between ourselves, quite as well as you or I). Let him get a taste of Buona Fortuna, — I have told you there is a limited supply, — who knows? He might insist on having it at the *prezzo discreto* he pays me for ordinary *vino da pasto*."

"Which is quite good enough for him," Patsy put in. "Trust me, mum's the word."

"Our cousin Roberto has come to say the requiem, Signora; will you stay for it?" Vittoria gravely invited.

It seemed better to go, hard as it was to drive back to Rome when we had meant to spend the morning at the *villino;* still, our visit was evidently ill timed, so we began to take leave, — a long business. Attilio cut a market basket full of roses for us; Vittoria added six fresh eggs from her own black Spanish hens. When I think of the brother and sister, it is as they were that morning, gathering fruit and flowers in the *villino* garden, creatures of an-

56

other world, estrays from the Golden Age. In
the city Attilio is dumb, shy, awkward ; on his
own ground he is a master of life. Tall, lean,
brown, with kind blue eyes, neatly cut mouth
and chin ; every wrinkle of his face is a line of
laughter, not one of care. He reads no newspapers, has no politics, no occupation, — beyond
the care of his vineyard, — is full of the wine
of human geniality, and is held, by grave Don
Manuel, Patsy, and others, one of the best com-
panions on earth. His man Belisario (always
at his heels) is curiously like him in looks
and manners ; the servant is a coarse copy
of the master. Attilio is *borghese,* Belisario
contadino.

Vittoria — exquisitely neat in a short white
linen skirt and jacket ; her wonderful dark hair
in heavy crisp masses, parted and coiled low at
the back of her head ; her cheeks the color
of the nectarines, her throat and hands hardly
paler than the warm tints of the apricots — is a
treasure of memory !

Belisario went to get our trap from the cool
grotto-like stable under the house. I followed

with sugar for Pegasus, Don Manuel's chestnut stallion. It was so dark in the stable that I stumbled and almost fell over some hard object that did not properly belong there.

" *Buona fortuna* " (good luck) " you did not hurt yourself over the garden roller, Signora," said Belisario, picking me up. He laughed as if he had said something funny. Seeing I was a little vexed by his laughter over a joke I could not understand, he carefully brushed the dust from my dress. Pegasus whinnied and put his pink velvet muzzle into my hand.

" Keep some sugar for the *asinello*, Signora ; he is really a better friend to us than Pegasus, he brings us *buona fortuna*. But go not near that devil mule ; it bites and kicks everybody but the Signorina Vittoria. She has a manner with animals ; you should see her charm the lizards."

The little gray donkey's stall was at the far end of the gloomy stable, close by a heavy door leading to the new wine-cellar Attilio and Belisario had been digging to store the wine

from Attilio's vineyard ; he supplies us, and
most of Don Manuel's friends (we form a little
cosmopolitan court around the great artist and
his lovely wife, the Signora Gemma).   Attilio,
too lazy to make friends on his own account,
annexes Don Manuel's ; they all adore him.

"How are you getting on with the wine-
cellar ? " I asked Belisario.

"Famously ! Would you like to see it ?
Here is the *padrone ;* he does not trust me with
a key."   At that moment Attilio and Patsy
came in.

"You wish to see the new cellar, Signora ?
But certainly, with pleasure."   He took a key
from a ring hanging at his belt and unlocked
the heavy doors, throwing them wide open.
It was a damp, earthy cavern, with vast
iron-bound casks ranged in tiers against the
walls.   At the further end was a low opening
leading, apparently, to some more distant cave.
Near this were several casks smaller than the
others ; they looked older and more carefully
made.

"What wine is this ? " I asked.

"That is the wine of Buona Fortuna, Signora; the same I advised our friend here not to speak of to Roberto or my other customers. The supply is small. I keep it for ourselves, and a few others able to appreciate it. 'T is too good a wine for the first comer."

" How far would it be to drive back to Rome by the via delle Tre Madonne ? " I asked Attilio.

" How far from here to Rome ? " Patsy interrupted. " Just two thousand years ! "

II

WE met them coming back from the festa of
the *Madonna del Divin' Amore*. Attilio was
driving the donkey in a small cart; Vittoria
and Patsy sat behind. She wore a wreath of
red artificial roses with silver paper leaves.
The donkey had bunches of carnations at his
ears, a garland of grape-leaves round his neck ;
the little cart was festive with flowers and
green boughs. I had been with the Signora
Gemma to make a formal call at the Spanish
embassy. She wore her diamond earrings and
her new French frock. I never saw her look
handsomer or more distinguished. We sat up
as straight as we could in the fine new victoria.
Pegasus was smartly groomed, the silver-
mounted harness shone. Belisario had on his
new livery, with a yellow cockade in his high
hat. Wagon and carriage stopped, Pegasus
whinnied, the donkey heehawed, Belisario
winked (I am sure of it, though his back was

rigid), the Signora Gemma flushed, Vittoria turned pale.

"After what Manuel said last year, you have been again to the festa of the *Divin' Amore*," said the Signora reproachfully.

"*Accipreti!*" cried Attilio, "*sorella mia*," (sister mine) "you take your pleasure, shall we not take ours?"

"What is there against the festa?" I asked.

"Our uncle the bishop does not like the children to go."

"Well, what can you expect of a Carmelite? Roberto, now, has never said anything against our going," argued Attilio.

The bishop is a strict churchman and an ascetic; priests of his stripe think the feast of the Divine Love is celebrated with too much of this world's good cheer. Roberto is a liberal; he accepts, if he does not endorse, the popular festival. The bishop is over seventy and thin-blooded; the priest is *bel 'uomo*, and not quite thirty years old.

The Signora Gemma drove me home. Patsy went back to the villino with Attilio and Vit-

toria. We did not see him for several days,
an unusual thing at that season. It was midsummer; our house was almost the last in the
Anglo-American Colony still open. Patsy
generally dropped in to dine on the terrace,
or afterwards to smoke his cigar and watch
Charles's Wain wheeling across the sky from
the Castel Sant' Angelo towards St. Peter's
dome.

" What happened after you got back to the
villino that day ? " I asked.

" Great work ! Padre Roberto came out
strong as a peacemaker. When peace was
proclaimed, he and I and Attilio made a night
of it. After all he said to me, Attilio could
not keep that wine (wherever he gets it, knocks
me) from the priest. Yes, we made a night of
it, — saving your presence, — we were all rather
the worse for wear. Roberto was billed to say
mass at five the next morning — it was the
anniversary of the day somebody belonging to
Don Manuel had been born, or married, or
died — and he had come out the night before
to be on hand. Attilio brought out a *fiascone*

of Buona Fortuna ; though it seems light, it is many times as strong as most wines. Attilio did not tell Roberto this, and we filled him up in great style, till he was as happy as a lord. It was nearly three o'clock when we broke up. Attilio had me out of bed again before five, to see how Roberto would say mass. Mind you, at three Roberto was reeling! The Signora Gemma was surprised to see Attilio and me come into the chapel, but she looked as pleased as Punch ; Don Manuel gave us an approving glance. Prompt to the minute Roberto came up to time, sober as a judge. He went through all his business uncommonly well, straight as a soldier. There was not a sign of the grape about him. After the service Roberto disappeared with a really grand benediction. The Signora kept us talking for a few minutes. When we got round to the sacristy the priest was gone ; his robe lay smoothly folded on a bench, everything was neat and regular. We went to Attilio's room ; there was Roberto fast asleep and snoring in the only spare bed — *my* bed ! He slept round the clock. I have seen an officer straighten up for drill, but not like Roberto; it was a miracle. When I talked with him about it the next day, what do you suppose he said ? ' The man fell from grace, not the priest.' "

" Are you not ashamed of yourself ? " I cried. Alas! I could get no confession of sin from Patsy.

When I next saw Attilio, he had a story to tell about Patsy.

" Perhaps you know, Signora, the Signorino Pattsi spent the night of the *Divin' Amore* at the *villino ?* "

" So he told me."

" Did he tell you how he got a bed to sleep in ? "

" No, he said nothing of that."

" It is to make laugh ! My quarters are in the studio building at the end of the garden. I have two rooms and two beds, — one for myself, one for a visitor. I had already invited my cousin Roberto to pass the night. The Signorino stayed rather late and took it into his head to sleep at the *villino*. I told him that it was too late to disturb the family in the big house and that I had but two beds in my rooms.

"'Then Roberto and I will play for that spare bed,' said Signorino Pattsi. 'Roberto, which am I thinking of, pink or blue?'

"'You are thinking of pink,' said poor Roberto.

"'You are wrong there, *caro mio*,' said the Signorino, 'I was thinking of blue.' And in one moment he was in Roberto's bed, sound asleep and snoring. *Questo giovine è matto*" (a mad fellow, that young man).

IV
THE CASTELLO

CHAPTER IV

THE CASTELLO

I

THE DREAM

IF Prince Montefiascone had not inter-
preted the dream, we should not have
had our *villeggiatura* at the Castello.
After June, July and August in Rome we
were a little weary of city life, — even of life
in the Eternal City. The Prince made an
offer of a large apartment in his castle (the
finest in Romagna), and J. quickly closed with
it, agreeing to pay one hundred and fifty francs
a month. When the Prince's steward brought
the lease, J. noticed that it was made out for
a rental of only seventy-five francs. He was
puzzled by this; but Attilio, who managed the
affair, said it was all right, so J. signed for
seventy-five, and paid one hundred and fifty in
advance. It was our first summer in Italy;

we knew less of such matters than we know now.

"Explain why the steward made me sign for half the amount I pay, if he does not pocket the difference?" J. demanded.

"*Ma chè!*" Attilio protested, "how can you be so suspicious? The man is perfectly honest, devoted to the Prince's interests. The paper you signed is to show the tax-collector, don't you see? They will only have to pay half the tax on that rent."

"Does the Prince approve?"

"The Prince probably knows nothing of it; he is always busy writing poetry and playing the piano."

We were all packed and ready to go next day, when I rode that dreadful gallop on the nightmare. In my dream we arrived at the flint-stone castle by the lake (it has five towers), crossed the bridge over the moat, passed through the low entrance, the square cortile, up the outer stair to our apartment, just as we had done the day we went to look at the place. There was only one difference: in the vast salon, barely furnished with a few *cinque cento* chairs, settles, and *cassoni*, stood two high black hearses or catafalques, with mourning hangings and sable ostrich plumes drooping from four funeral urns ; *they* were not there on our first visit. I woke cold with fright, convinced the dream was a warning that we should meet our deaths at the Castello. While the spell of the dream was still upon me, a card was brought in.

" Prince Montefiascone has called, " said J., and went to meet him. The Prince's manners were beautiful ; so were his eyes, large and pleading, like a stricken stag's. He looked a creature all nerves and spirit, so gentle and *simpatico* that before I knew it I had told him my dream, and my fear of the Castello.

" A strange dream indeed, Signora ; could it have anything to do with the discovery of the oubliette, I wonder ? " said the Prince.

" Oubliette, — where, when ? "

" While we were making some repairs at the Castello last week, we came upon a secret vault under a trap-door in your tower, and I am sorry to say found in it the skeletons of many unfortunate people who had met their death there. I spoke to Padre Roberto, the village priest, and a few nights after he sent two wagons to carry away the bones of those poor unfortunates, — may they rest in peace ! I am glad the Padre had the heart to bury them in the consecrated earth brought back from Palestine (as a penance) by the Monte-fiascone of the third crusade."

" Do you suppose the penance was for murdering the poor people ? Those two wagons were my two catafalques ; now I shall not be afraid to go to the Castello !"

We took possession of our apartment that afternoon. We had not been there an hour when Belisario drove up with donkey and donkey cart, bringing supplies of wine, oil, eggs, butter and poultry. Attilio had undertaken to provision us during our *villeggiatura.* Later, Vittoria, Attilio and Patsy arrived to help us establish ourselves, — they are the kindest people in the world !

My den was in the tower, — just a little circu-

72

lar room, with a low door giving upon a most darling garden within the castle wall. Vittoria immediately set to work tidying up the tiny garden. The box border on either side of the path had grown out of all bounds; it met in the middle. She had brought a pair of shears and set to work to clip away the branches from the walk. Patsy, pretending to help, really hindered her.

" Vittoria, do you remember how it feels to live inside a tree ? " he asked.

" No, it would be impossible for me to remember. I never have lived inside a tree."

" Yes, you have! How else should you know so much about trees and weeds and flowers ? Belisario says you can make anything grow ; you 're a dryad ! "

She smiled at him indulgently.

" What is this tree ? " I asked.

" The Judas tree," said Vittoria. " Do you know how it got its name ? In the Garden of Gethsemane grew a beautiful tree covered with white flowers. When Judas entered the garden and betrayed his Master with a kiss, the tree blushed for shame. It blushes still, and will do so till the end of the world."

" It was the goat told Vittoria all those things that make her so clever," said Attilio.

" What goat ? Tell us," Patsy exclaimed.

" An old nanny-goat with yellow hair and eyes, — that's where Vittoria got *her* eyes. Our poor mother (of blessed memory) died when Vittoria was born. Gemma was fifteen and I was ten at the time, so I remember it well. There being no woman in the village with milk to spare, my father trained a milch goat to give suck to the poor baby. At nursing time he rang a bell, and good old nanny-goat trotted into the house, found baby in the cradle, and gave her the teat. Oh, yes, if you had seen Vittoria when she was *so* high, you would have known her for a goat's weanling. She used to shake her little head and caper, like a kid. She has it in her blood. The Signorino is right ; she is a wild piece."

Vittoria on her knees training a coral honey-suckle round a stone sun-dial, a wisp of straw

for tying the vine in her mouth, only murmured, "*stia zitto!*" (be silent).

"Why is nothing planted on this side of the
castle?" I asked Attilio. The fields on the
right were full of standing oats, tall flax, and
barley; the land on the left lay fallow.

"The Prince has so much land," Attilio explained, "that he divides it in five parts, and
plants each part in turn. It is because the land
is only planted one year out of five and rests the
other four that he always has such fine crops."

"Did you ever hear of phosphates, Attilio?"
Patsy asked.

"What are they, Signora?"—Attilio appealed to me,—"a new kind of grain?"

"If you were a decent Roman citizen you
wouldn't ask," Patsy derided. "You would go
into the senate every day and cry, 'Reclaim
the Campagna!' like that old bore Cato with
his '*delenda est Carthago.*' Plants every five
years! That's because time is the only 'en-
richer' they know. No hurry about things here,
is there? Perhaps that's part of the magic."

"It *is* the magic."

A few days after we were comfortably settled, the Prince moved into his wing of the Castello. Patsy, who was staying with us (he was already the Prince's intimate friend), took a hand in Montefiascone's removal from the Roman palazzo to the Castello, — a simple enough affair. Two prehistoric trunks, a bed, a bath-tub, an Erard piano, some kitchen utensils and provisions came out from Rome in an immense wagon drawn by four oxen, — proud creatures with terrible horns, angry eyes and sleek gray coats; they showed breeding and race quite as much as their owner. We were all sitting in the loggia outside Montefiascone's library, when we heard the creak, creak, of the heavy wheels, the sighs of the oxen, as they strained up the steep flagged way leading to the cortile; their broad breasts heaved, they savagely flicked away the flies with their mighty tails as they came to a standstill, lowing sullenly.

"Let's come down and help unload," said Patsy.

"Too hot," the Prince objected; "there are enough of them without us."

"Oh, come on!" Patsy was off like a flash of lightning.

"Some gadfly stings him, eh? He always itches to be doing," said the Prince. "Look at him lifting off that heavy cover they put over the cart to keep out the dust of the road."

Patsy stripped off the cover, threw it on the ground, began to fold it up, stopped, unrolled it, turned it over, gave a long whistle, and sat down suddenly. After a moment, apparently of stupefaction, he roared, wildly waving his arms: "Come down, come down all of you and see what I have found!" We came down the long stairs slowly (it was still hot), and stood beside him.

"Well?" said Montefiascone.

Patsy unrolled the cover. "Is this the best use you have for your old Flemish tapestries? I could find a better," he said.

"Where did you get this from?" asked the Prince of the contadino who drove the oxen.

"From the loft, where such things are kept, Excellency."

"Have you used it before in this way?"

"We always use it, *Illustrissimo;* there are others, but this is the best."

"How many others?"

"Four, six, ten, — how do I know? There are always enough to cover the carts when we move."

"Yes, they make good cart covers," said the Prince, "but I have a fancy to use this one in another manner. Get a broom, sweep it carefully; when it is clean bring it up to the library."

"Do you know," Patsy asked, when the magnificent old tapestry was spread out on the library floor, "what that furniture covering of yours is worth?"

"No, I have not an idea."

"Five thousand scudi at the lowest figure, without a stitch of repair. Properly restored, it will be worth double. Four, six, ten others did he say? Man! You have found a fortune to-day!"

"You have brought me the good fortune," said the Prince, quite shaken. He is said to be in dreadful straits for money.

"Don't mention it," cried Patsy; then to me in an undertone: "His cook has n't come, do ask him to dinner to-night."

"Pray don't incommode yourself, Signora," the Prince began; "my supper is the simplest affair."

"Ours is n't," interrupted Patsy. "Not to-night! May n't we celebrate finding those tapestries? Whom can we invite? Let's send for Vittoria and Attilio." J. touched him warningly.

"Why do you kick me?" asked Patsy; then, understanding: "No, Montefiascone would not like to dine with our wine-merchant and his sister. What a bore it must be to be an aristocrat!"

"An original, our Pattsi, eh? What energy! — I should like to buy him," murmured the Prince.

Montefiascone dined with us; he seemed as much pleased with our pleasure in the rooms that were ours for a few weeks, and his for life, as Patsy himself.

"This is the right sort of dining-room," cried

Patsy. " Gothic roof, stone floor, wax candles in silver candlesticks, roses in a Venetian glass. The rest does n't matter. Luxury is the only thing it is degrading to do without. In your family, Prince, where tapestries are only good enough for cart covers, that is understood. I know a fellow who would like to get hold of those rags of yours — he 'd give you any price — money is of no object."

" Thank you kindly," said the Prince. I have looked up the matter in the archives, — they are kept out here in the library. That tapestry is one of a set of seven given to one of my ancestors by Pope Sixtus Fifth. They represent scenes from the history of the Monte-fiasconi ; it would be a pity to let them go out of the family, don't you think, Signora ? "

" How could such things be lost sight of ? " I exclaimed.

" Oh, things, things ! There are so many ! The top story of the palazzo is like a big anti-quarian's shop. Nothing is ever given away or destroyed. Whenever we refurnish, the dis-carded things are carried upstairs ; there are

pictures, mirrors, furniture, every fashion of the
last three hundred years. My poor mother is
an invalid, she has only my brother and me ;
neither of us takes much interest in such
matters."

We learned later that the Principessa was
hopelessly insane, that neither son could remember her in any other state, that they devoted their lives to caring for her, and that one
or the other was always with her.

"What wine is this?" asked the Prince,
looking at me.

" A present from the Signorino."

" You like it ? " Patsy asked.

The Prince held his glass to the light, smelled
the wine, and tasted it again. " It suits me
very well," he said. " You spoke of your wine-
merchant — "

" I think well of that wine, myself," Patsy
interrupted.

" Would you mind telling me where it comes
from ? "

" Not in the least, my dear fellow, if I only
knew."

TWO IN ITALY

" What is it called ? "

" Buona Fortuna."

" *Un vino famoso !* The taste seems familiar,
— I could almost fancy I know the vineyard, —
but no, it is not possible ! "

" Have another glass ? " said Patsy.

II

"*Diamine!* My son, you should have it if I could get it for you," said Attilio, " but I tell you, *parola d' onore* it is finished. You have had the last *gocciatino* of Buona Fortuna you will ever taste."

" What 's happened ? You can't wipe out a vineyard by battle, murder, or plague," Patsy objected.

" *E vero*, but, take my word for it, you have drained the last glass that will pass your lips."

" So you said." Patsy is tenacious. " If the wine exists, I shall find it. Since for you ' it is finished,' why not tell me where you got it from ? "

Attilio was obstinately silent.

" Look here, Attilio; there 's some hocus-pocus about Buona Fortuna ; there has been a mystery about it from the first. Whatever it is, Belisario knows. Now, as man to man,

83

shall I buy the secret of him, or will you tell
me ? "

" Useless to spend good money on that ugly
hangman. If I tell you, will you promise to
act as if you did not know ? That 's my
condition."

" *Benone*, go ahead."

" One morning, while we were at work digging the new wine-cellar at the *villino* — at
least Belisario was at work — I had stepped
out to draw a breath, when I heard him cry
out as if something wonderful had happened.
I hurried back to the cellar. 'What have
you found ? ' I asked.

" ' Only one of the catacombs of the ancient
Romans,' said Belisario. In digging he had come
upon an underground tunnel high enough for a
tall man to stand up in, nine or ten feet wide.

" ' There is no catacomb in this part of the
country that I ever heard of ; it is a great discovery,' I said. ' The ancients often buried
precious things with their dead, who knows ?
We may find a treasure of gold and jewels.
Be careful not to speak of this.' You, Signor-

ino, are the first to hear the tale. Belisario
has not spoken for fear of his precious skin.
The first thing was to explore the catacomb.
We decided it was best for Belisario to go
alone, for me to remain and guard the secret
in case any one should come. He took a
lantern, matches, and a ball of twine. I stood
at the opening holding the clue. '*In bocca
al lupo*' (in the mouth of the wolf), I said to
give him courage. Belisario started. He is
not afraid of man nor devil. I watched his
light grow smaller and smaller. Now and
again he twitched the cord ; one pull meant
' all right,' two, ' I have found something,'
three, ' danger.' Suddenly the light disappeared, the rope twitched once. I knew that
Belisario had turned a corner. I waited a
long time ; then I knew by the feeling that
he was rolling up the clue and returning. He
came back, his eyes big and scared.

" ' What have you found, — any tombs ? ' I
asked.

" ' No,' said Belisario, ' no tombs. I do not
believe it is a catacomb ; it may be only one

of the tunnels, left by the ancients and forgotten, for getting out the *pozzolana*' (a red earth, used to mix with mortar). 'The cord gave out. I must take a longer one, but not to-day.'

"The next morning Belisario tried again, taking a second ball of twine in his pocket. When he came to the end of the first, he spliced the two, and went twice as far as the day before ; still he found nothing. The third day he took about a mile of cord. After waiting a long time the clue twitched twice. I knew Belisario had found something. You may be sure I was in a hurry to see that sheep's face of his. He came back, his eyes bigger than ever.

" '*Padrone !*' he cried, 'a miraculous thing has happened ; the passage ends as it begins, — in a wine-cellar ! '

" 'You are mad or lying ! '

" 'Come and see. There is an immense cellar ; doubtless it belonged to one of the Roman Emperors, perhaps to the great Augusto. The casks are very old ; there are even some amphoræ in the more distant part.'

86

THE CASTELLO

"I felt sure he was not speaking the truth; to prove it I went back with him. It was just as he had said: the cellar was even bigger, — half as large as the crypt of St. Peter's, — and there was wine enough for an army of Austrians. After all our fatigue we were naturally thirsty; we had taken so much trouble to find that cave, we certainly had a right to taste the wine; we tapped a cask (it had been tapped before; Belisario had helped himself, though he swore he had not). In that immense cavern, really a magnificent chamber with columns cut out of the soft clay, I drained my first glass of that peerless wine. 'This is *buona fortuna*, Belisario,' I said; 'far better than gold or jewels, for a cup of this makes a man feel as if he owned all the gold and jewels in the world!'

"'*Buona fortuna* indeed!' said Belisario; so the wine got its name. 'It is a pity,' I said, 'that we cannot take back a little; it is doing nobody any good here.'

"'It is a thousand pities,' he agreed.

"'Wastefulness is a sin my cousin Roberto

has often warned us against ; it is a pure waste
to let this splendid wine lie here idle, when
it might be nourishing good men and giving
them power to do good works. It is our duty
to stop this waste; let us go back, and get
some *fiasconi.*' He assented. As we came out
of the darkness, Belisario blinking his bat's
eyes at the light, what should we see but the
garden roller? It has a pair of iron shafts
and two pointed pieces of iron which hold the
stone roller in place.

" ' *Corpo di Baccho !* ' I exclaimed ; ' that
roller is just the size of those casks.' Belisario
understood.

" ' Yes,' he said ; ' we can take out the stone
roller and fasten the barrel in its place; but,
padrone, it will be heavy to draw, the ground
of the tunnel is very uneven.'

" ' Imbecile ! what is that ass standing there
for ? The wine will be a lighter load than the
granite roller, too heavy for any animal except
that preposterous mule, a creature without
pride of ancestry or hope of progeny.'

" *Povero asinello*, he was at first frightened,

but soon became accustomed to the darkness. We reached the ancient cave safely, stuck the two sharpened points of the iron which hold the stone, into the ends of a cask, — it was just the right size. We started ; the barrel turned on its side, round and round like a wheel; in this way we dragged it to our own cellar. I let it stand a week to allow the wine to settle, then opened the cask. You tasted the second flask, Signorino. I have shared fairly with you for the sake of your appreciation of fine wine."

"You are too good; I wish you had n't," Patsy groaned.

"*And* your independence of it," Attilio continued. "I swear by all the saints never before knew I a man who could drink water, and even milk — *milk*, and keep health and spirits as if properly nourished by the wine Papà Baccho provided for us."

"*Grazie mille;* what next ? "

"*Niente !* And there was enough to last us all our lives. A week ago, 'twas after I sent that supply to the Castello, we needed a new cask. Belisario departed as usual with the *asinello;* he comes back, his stupid face blank as that wall. 'What has happened?' I cried; 'where is the wine?'

" 'No more Buona Fortuna for us,' he said; 'the cave is bricked up!' "

" The Emperor Augustus was not the owner?" said Patsy.

" I erred in judgment. · The owner, may he die of an apoplexy, is evidently alive."

"And has discovered the theft."

" Apparently. It is a great misfortune; we must accept it. As I told you, it is finished."

" Finished? You will be had up for theft."

" What a child you are! Belisario worked day and night, — that fellow is a clever *muratore,* — you would swear the wall at our end was twenty years old. We burned the casks; where is the evidence?"

" I suppose I am an accomplice after the theft."

" Understand, what a man finds in the bowels of the earth or the depths of the ocean is not like that which is above ground; it is treasure trove. The wine was ours, as the pearls of the sea are the diver's who risks his life for them."

" Whose cellar was it ? "

" Who knows ? One who can well afford to lose a few paltry casks of wine."

" Give me the points of the compass and the direction and I will soon find out."

" *Lascia andare!* (leave things as they are). The owner was careless; it is damnable to put temptation in men's way; he has but himself to thank. If we had only taken a few more casks ! "

III

" I SHOULD be only too glad to have you remain another month if you do not mind being here on the fifteenth," said the Prince.

" What happens then ? " asked J.

" It is the festa of Santa Sabina d' Anticoli. Many people come to the Castello. To reach the chapel, where the miracle took place, they pass up your stairs ; I feared the noise might disturb you."

" A saint, a crusader, and an oubliette, — what else has he up his sleeve ? " murmured Patsy.

" What was the miracle ? " J. politely asked.

" Santa Sabina raised the head of the house from the dead."

" Was the saint a member of his family ? "

" His sister. It is all set down in the archives. Padre Roberto can tell you more than I. She founded a convent in Spain, and was canonized by Papa Sisto Quinto."

"Pope Sixtus seems to have been quite a friend of the family," said Patsy.

"He was undoubtedly our greatest benefactor," the Prince replied, as gravely as if the benefits had been conferred yesterday.

Of course we decided to stay. The celebration began on the *vigilia ;* from the afternoon of the fourteenth till the evening of the fifteenth, cortile and stair were black with people coming and going. We met the Signora Gemma and Vittoria outside the chapel door.

"This, Signora, is what the box that grows in your garden is used for. I hope I did not clip away too much," said Vittoria. "How good it smells!"

The chapel floor — it was paved with *rosso antico* and *paonazetto* — was strewn with twigs of green box ; trodden under the people's feet, it gave out a delicious bitter odor, that, mingled with the incense, filled the Castello.

"Will you go down into the confessio and see the head of Santa Sabina?" asked the Signora Gemma.

"No, *cara*," Vittoria interrupted ; "to them

it would not be a pleasure. Let us look rather at these splendid curtains; who would believe they could be made of straw?" The walls were covered with curious hangings of warm gold color, rich and beautiful.

"They were made in Spain by the nuns of Santa Sabina's convent; they are *oggetti unici*, none others in the world; they are three hundred years old, and may be seen only on this one day of all the year."

At the head of the stairs stood a vast ancient Roman porphyry vase filled with small branches of olive. The Signora dipped her fingers in a silver holy-water vessel, and offered them for us to touch. Vittoria gave us each an olive branch; all who came down the stair carried a spray of the pretty gray-green leaves.

"Have you called yet upon the Prince?" asked the Signora.

"No; have you?"

"We are not going. The chapel is open to all the world to-day; only the Prince's friends are expected to call on him; you should go.

If you see my cousin Roberto, tell him we are here."

We found Montefiascone in his library. Patsy had that moment come in.

" Here you are at last ! " said the Prince. "I have looked for you; they are all gone now, *grazie Deo*, except Padre Roberto. How many visitors, Padre ? "

" Half of Rome, it appears to me."

" *Caro* Pattsi, how do your tapestries look ? "

" I say ! are n't they ripping ? The gorgeous carved ceiling, the fine pavement, and the walls left bare for this sort of thing. If you ever sell them, Montefiascone, I 'll cut you."

" I stood here to receive my guests, before this tapestry. You recognize the subject ? "

" It 's the miracle ! There 's your many times great-grandfather, there 's Santa Sabina, there — why, it 's the Castello in the background; I can even make out the five towers and the lake."

" With your permission, Signora." The host threw himself down on the settle beside me. " I have stood since early this morning. A glass of wine and a bit of *pizza ?* Carolina, *per carità, un bicchiere di vino !*"

The old cook hobbled in with a tray of glasses, a silver flagon, and a huge *panettone di Milano.*

"*Grazie;* hand it to the Signorino and to Padre Roberto." The two men looked at the Prince as they raised their glasses. "*A vostra Eccellenza !*" said Padre Roberto, bowing with the splendid grace of the Italian clerico.

" Here's hoping — " Patsy began ; he drank a little wine, then set down the glass, gave his familiar long low whistle of surprise, and looked hard at Padre Roberto ; a spark of recognition flashed between them.

" This is a great wine," said Patsy.

"*Famoso !*" the priest agreed, tasting it again.

" Would you mind telling me where you get it from, Prince ?" Patsy asked.

" From my vineyard, — where else ?" said Montefiascone, surprised at the question. To him it was as much a matter of course that a man should own his vineyard as that he should own his bed.

" *Beato voi* to possess such a vineyard !   Do you make more wine than you use ? "

" Oh, yes ; we sell a small amount every year."

" May I become one of your customers ? "

" *Altro che!* of course.   I will speak to the steward about it.   He was complaining the other day that last year's vintage was the smallest he had ever known, but for you there will always be enough."

Patsy held his glass to the light, sighed deeply, then turned and looked at the seven splendid tapestries of Papa Sisto.

" After all, I found the tapestries for you ! " he said, as if pleading extenuation for some hidden crime against his friend.

Montefiascone threw an arm over Patsy's shoulder, — but for his cleverness in avoiding the embrace would have kissed him Latin fashion, on either cheek.

" I shall always owe you a debt for that, *amico mio!*" said the Prince.

Patsy nodded, apparently consoled. "It was a wonderful piece of luck, — what you call *buona fortuna*, was n't it?"

"Stupendous!" said Padre Roberto.

"Miraculous!" murmured the Prince.

"Padre, the Signora Gemma and Vittoria are here —" I began, suddenly remembering the message.

"Where?" stormed Patsy, putting down his glass and rushing from the library; "you might have said so before!"

"Where is he going?" Montefiascone asked.

"To Vittoria."

"*Beato lui!*" said the Prince.

Padre Roberto sighed, finished his glass of wine slowly, and followed. At the library door he paused, looked back, and smiled kindly to us all as he said:

"*Arrivederci amici, e buona notte!*"

V

SAVONAROLA FINNERTY

(WHAT I HEARD OF HIM)

CHAPTER V

SAVONAROLA FINNERTY

(WHAT I HEARD OF HIM)

I

OUT OF THE FRYING PAN

PATSY lived in the Via Flaminia. He had the whole ground floor of an old house not far from the Porta del Popolo. There was one large room where he worked, with a balcony at the end where he and his brown and white pointer puppy slept. A smaller room with a concrete floor served as a salon. Here, on an old *cassone*, stood a *quarternóla* of the wine of Buona Fortuna. The salon opened upon an enclosed garden, one of whose walls was covered with climbing tea-roses, another by a mass of trained heliotrope. At the angle where the two walls met stood an ancient fountain, green with moss, water plants, and the feathery fern that loves damp places and is called the hair of Venus

103

Patsy's garden was a pleasant place ; his salon was accounted by the group of artists and *literati* who made it their rendezvous, "the coolest thing in Rome." Here, the day's work over, Patsy, Savonarola Finnerty, and Attilio sat discussing the scant midsummer news and the merits of Buona Fortuna. It was that black cholera summer, when the people died like sheep in Naples, and all of Italy was under the ban of fear. There were no tourists that year, and few of the foreigners who could afford to get out of Rome remained in the city.

"You have heard about the Pope's manifesto?" asked Finnerty; "he has put by a million francs to be spent for the sick if the cholera comes to Rome."

"Ah," sighed Attilio, "he is a good man. Perhaps we were better off in the old days." Though Attilio cared nothing about politics, he inclined to the liberal side. It was one of those periodical moments of discontent with the Government, when the economical asked if the price of liberty had not come too high.

"That only means they 've been down on you

for your taxes," said Patsy. "When I was at the station this morning I saw the king's train pull out. There was a car-kitchen filled with food, pots, pans, and cooks. Hitched on behind was a great water-tank filled with *Acqua di Trevi.*"

"Where was he going with all that *roba ?*" (stuff).

"To Naples to meet King Cholera! To visit the sick in the hospitals. While Leo waits — keeping back his million-franc trump, Umberto takes the trick."

"I would not go to Naples *now* to be made Emperor of the world," said Finnerty. "It's tempting Providence, even, to stay in Rome. The French newspapers say the cholera's already here."

"Only one case, — a man who came from Naples. He was spotted, and isolated immediately. The doctors say there's no danger of its spreading."

"Come to Venice with me," urged Finnerty; "what's the use of waiting here, flattening our noses against the gates of the Protestant cemetery ?"

"If you will do as I tell you," said Attilio, impressively, "you need have no fear of cholera. Eat for your breakfast every morning *pane arrosto ed aglio*" (toast and garlic). "The bread must be toasted very hard; then take a clove of garlic, and, using the toast as a nutmeg-grater, rub the garlic well into it; with a little oil, pepper, and salt, it's not bad, I assure you, a sort of bread salad. Drink, with this, a little good red wine that has turned to vinegar, in a glass of water, and you'll be quite safe."

"Where did you learn that?" asked Patsy.

"It's a priest's trick, — a precaution against contagion. I had it from Padre Roberto."

"Even a cholera germ hates the smell of garlic! I have told Pietro, if he does n't give up eating it I'll discharge him," groaned Patsy; "and now you're putting Savo' up to eating the vile stuff."

Pietro, the jail-bird who took care of Patsy's apartment, was outside in the garden. He looked up from the remains of a huge watermelon he was gobbling noisily, and grinned at the mention of his name. He had scooped out the seeds and filled the melon with *acqua-vite*. "Look at him!" said Patsy, "and listen to him. Pietro, where did that fine melon come from?"

"Oh, I got it," Pietro answered vaguely.

"From the *fruttajuolo del Re?*" Pietro laughed and nodded.

"Then you stole it," Patsy accused.

"No, no, Signorino; am I a thief? I found it, yes. You do not believe? Then go out to the Campagna, beyond the Porta Paulo, and you will find a mountain of them, and many other splendid fruits and vegetables besides. But, *magari!* you cannot eat them. What do you think? The *guardie* destroyed cartloads of these excellent fruits this morning. First they made a pile of them, then poured on an abomination called quicklime. I waited till the *guardie* had gone, then poked with a stick into the pile and found, at the bottom, this admirable melon, hardly contaminated by that outrageous stuff. Is it not a shame, I ask you, when so many are hungry, to destroy the good fruits the blessed saints have sent us?"

107

" What can it mean ? " Patsy exclaimed.

" The municipality seizes and destroys all unripe or over-ripe fruit," said Attilio. " Moreover, it floods the market with lemons sold at cost price. I never remember them so cheap. It is necessary for the preservation of the health through the hot weather — especially in a cholera season — that the people should consume many lemons."

" And in New York," murmured Patsy, " we throw cartloads of peaches into the East River to keep up the market price ! "

" There 's something to be said for a paternal government, after all," Finnerty admitted. " What Attilio says about the lemons and destroying the fruit decides me. I 'm off for Venice to-night. Who comes with me ? "

" But why to Venice ? " said Attilio. " The people there are perfidious."

" Who comes with me ? Going, going — "

" Beware of the Venetians ! " Attilio implored.

" Going — gone ! "

Savonarola went alone.

II

It was Finnerty's first season in Italy. His knowledge of the language was limited. He could swear at cabmen and waiters, he could read the bill of fare at a restaurant.

Outside the railroad station at Venice he hailed a bronzed gondolier dressed in dark blue flannel with a red sash. "You're a good-looking chap — seem to have a nice gondola. What's your name? *Come se chiama*, eh?"

"Raffredo, si'or. Hotel Daniele, sir?"

"No — too dear, *troppo caro*. Lodgings — bed — sleep." Closing his eyes, Finnerty laid his head on his hand. "Then American consul."

"*Va bene, si'or, ho capito.* Lodgin' *camere mobiliate, poi al consolo Americano.*"

"You'll do. Go ahead!" Finnerty leaned back against the leather cushions of the gondola's black *felze* (cabin), abandoning himself to the joy of a first row on the Grand Canal. The swish-swash of the oar, the melancholy

cries of the gondoliers, "*Stai oh! sa premi!*"
were music after eighteen hours of the loco-
motive's screech and the tara-tara of the train
guard's horn. The changing color, the poetry,
the charm of Venice swept over him, a warm
wave of delight. He forgot the ugly fear of
cholera that had driven him from Rome to
the opal city of the lagoons.

"What a model that fellow would make!"
said Finnerty. "He has the head, torso,
arms, legs — everything." He made a note in
his sketch-book of the gondolier's pose.

Though Raffredo was well acquainted with
young artists and their vagaries of dress, even
he was impressed by his fare's appearance.
"*Un bel giovine, ma molto originale*" (a handsome young man, but very original), he said
to his wife that night. Finnerty's was a
dashing, brilliant personality; he was tall and
handsome, with a shock of chestnut curls, and
bright blue eyes. He wore a pea-green cut-
away coat, having two peculiar metal buttons
at the back, with trousers to match, made
from his own design. Close fitting from waist

to knee, below the knee they became leggings
fastened together with hooks and eyes. His
curious pointed shoes were of soft brown
leather; his hat, a black felt sombrero, had
the eye of a peacock feather tucked in the
band. Finnerty was a full-blooded Irishman,
"American born;" he had the Celtic temper-
ament and the American point of view.

At that time the American consulate occupied the *piano nobile* of an old Venetian palace.
The windows gave on a small triangular garden, with a balcony at the end commanding a
view of the Grand Canal and the church of
Santa Maria della Salute.

"Is the consul at home?" Finnerty asked
the young man he found in the dingy office.

"He is out of town. I represent him.
What can I do for you?"

"The vice-consul, I suppose?"

"Officially, no; practically, I serve my uncle
in that capacity."

"You can understand me — that's something. My name's Savonarola Finnerty; perhaps you've heard of me?"

111

"Pleased to meet you, Mr. Finnerty. An artist? Travelling for pleasure? Delightful city this, full of color and that sort of thing."

"Any cholera here?" asked Finnerty, suddenly remembering his errand.

"Only four cases."

Finnerty dropped into a chair, dashed his feathered hat to the ground, and swore long and furiously. The consul's nephew, a tiny caricature of a man, with fair hair parted in the middle, put a square monocle (it had a black vulcanite frame and was attached to a dark ribbon) in his left eye, and looked at Finnerty. The monocle was made of plain glass and magnified nothing but the little man's importance. He rose, glanced at himself in the mirror, twirled his cane, a short malacca joint with a silver knob at each end, and threw open a door leading to the garden.

"Come outside — it's cooler — and have a smoke. My name's de Ruyter Ruby, of Boisé City, Idaho."

"Wish I was there now — wish I was in any other d— place but this!" wailed Finnerty.

SAVONAROLA FINNERTY

"Venice is not so bad; you'll like it after a week," said Mr. Ruby, soothingly. There were white and purple stocks, mignonette, and pink roses in the consul's garden. Finnerty strode restlessly up and down, stopped before a blush-rosebush, mechanically picked off a snail that was devouring a bud, pulled up a weed, — it was strangling a half-opened lily, — caught a spray of green leaves between his fingers, rubbed it in the palm of his hand, and smelt of it.

"Why, this is mint!" he exclaimed.

"No! Real mint? American mint? I never knew it grew here," said the consul's nephew.

Finnerty looked at him with the scorn of one who uses his eyes for one who only sees with them.

"Real American mint; it reminds me of home. It's the season for mint-juleps." Finnerty sighed deeply.

"I've not tasted a mint-julep since I left Boisé City, two years ago. I forget how they're made," said Mr. Ruby.

"Pounded ice, mint, sugar, cognac — or whatever liquor you prefer. I used to mix a good one."

"There's a bottle of Bourbon inside — "

"Cognac's better. 'Fine champagne,' or 'three stars' would do."

"If I had anybody to send — the boy's out — "

"There's the fellow with the gondola — name is Raffredo — "

"I'll send him to the English pharmacy for some brandy. It won't take him ten minutes to get it. While we're waiting, would you like to see the last New York papers? They came only this morning. I have not had time to open the mail to-day."

"*Papers?* No, thank you. Where do you keep the ice? I'll begin by pounding it."

Mr. Ruby brought out a block of ice, a hammer, and a napkin. The next half-hour was profitably employed in preparing the mint-julep. When it was ready, Ruby and Finnerty seated themselves on either side of a table bearing a large glass jug filled with tinkling ice, sprays of fragrant mint, and the best "fine champagne."

"You're an artist at mixing drinks, Mr. Finnerty. This is the best mint-julep I ever tasted."

"Thank you. How comfortable this shaker rocking-chair is! I wish I had one in Rome."

The soothing effects of the mint-julep soon showed themselves: Finnerty's views brightened ; acquaintance mellowed into friendship.

"You like living in Venice, Mr. Ruby ?"

"Well, — of course there's a lot of responsibility connected with my position, but as a first appointment I don't mind it, when the Missis is away."

"Your aunt ?"

"My uncle's wife. She was a de Ruyter of New York, an old Dutch family. When I entered diplomacy, I felt my name was not suited to the career. Timothy Ruby isn't a name for the diplomatic circle. I dropped Timothy and added de Ruyter — de Ruyter Ruby — sounds well, doesn't it ?"

"Oh, it's all right — better than mine.

What do you think of Martin Luther Savonarola Finnerty ? "

" It 's a shame ! Parents ought n't to be
allowed to saddle a fellow with such a name.
Why don't you change it ? "

" Oh, I don't know — my father gave it to
me, so I guess it will have to do. I only use
the Martin Luther for best, — on holidays and
Sundays. I say — *what* a sunset ! "

In the west the sun was going down wrapped
in a glory of crimson and gold ; the full moon
was rising in the east ; half the world was gold,
half silver.

" The Queen of the Adriatic is doing her
prettiest for you, Mr. Finnerty. This is the
finest sunset I have seen since I left home."

" Look at that moon ! I suppose the reason she 's so much more beautiful than the
sun is that she is of no earthly use," said Finnerty.

The mint-julep in the jug steadily decreased.
Some glimmering of discretion warned Mr.
Ruby that he had had enough.

" Excuse me, Finnerty," he said. " I must

attend to some important official business. Make yourself at home."

When the jug was quite empty, Finnerty re-entered the office. The door of an inner room was ajar; there, lying upon a sofa, he saw the consul's representative, a newspaper spread over his head to keep off the flies.

" Ah," sighed Finnerty, " in that julepous condition I won't wake you. See you later, old chap."

Forgetting Raffredo and the gondola (waiting for him at the main entrance), Finnerty passed out of the consulate by a side door into one of the dark labyrinthine *calli* (side streets) behind the palazzo. He meandered happily through the maze till, attracted by the sounds of music, he suddenly turned from a dim narrow lane into the Piazza San Marco. The great square was brilliantly lighted and crowded with people. Outside Florian's Café, gayly dressed ladies and splendid officers (laced and gold-laced) were seated at little tables consuming ices and black coffee. A pretty American girl was scattering corn for the pigeons;

117

their white wings fluttered about her head; they alighted fearlessly on her shoulders and fed from her hands.

"Venus and her doves," murmured Finnerty. He had the sense to give his fair compatriot a wide berth, and made his way to the middle of the Piazza, where the crowd was thickest round the band-stand. The musicians struck up a pot-pourri of American and Irish airs: "Hail Columbia," "The Harp that once through Tara's Halls," "Yankee Doodle," "Marching through Georgia," "The Suwanee River." Finnerty sang them all under his breath, keeping his eye on the majestic band-master who marked the time. The tune changed from "Home, Sweet Home" to "The Wearing of the Green." At the slogan of his race, passionate memories stirred:

"Oh, Paddy dear, and did you hear the news that's going
    round?

.   .   .   .

   They're hanging men and women there for wearing of
    the green!"

sang Finnerty at the top of his voice, "letting

out" whoop after whoop of the old Donny-
brook Fair order.

"Erin go bragh!" He cut a pigeon-wing,
danced a few steps of an Irish jig, slipped, fell,
and lay on the ground groaning with the pain
of hitting his head against the marble pavement. At that moment the medley ended with
a variation of "Dixie." In the comparative
silence that followed, Finnerty's groans were
heard, his hopeless efforts to get to his feet
observed. Then the one ominous voice in
every crowd cried, "Cholera!"

There was a moment of terrified silence, — a
panic, a wild stampede. The musicians fled, in-
struments in hand ; the trombone to the north,
French horn to the south, hautboy and cym-
bals east and west. Five minutes later Finnerty was alone in the Piazza with the pigeons,
the stars, and the four golden horses that
guard the entrance to the church of San
Marco. Perfectly conscious of what was hap-
pening, he lay as one paralyzed, unable to
speak or move. After a time he heard footsteps. He was lifted gently from the stones of

119

Venice (he found them hard), placed in an ambulance gondola, and rowed away to dreamland. Later he was conscious of being taken from the ambulance, carried through a dark passage to a large room, and put into a bed so comfortable that he did not trouble himself to ask questions, but, turning on his side with a drowsy "*buona notte*," fell sound asleep.

He was waked by some one gently placing a clinical thermometer in his mouth. He sat up in bed, wider awake than he had ever been in his life, and looked into the eyes of a very clean young man dressed in white linen.

"What's the meaning of this?" cried Finnerty."

"*Un momento.*"

"I want to get up —"

"*Stià tranquillo*" (be quiet), said the young man, firmly replacing the thermometer. Finnerty fell back on the pillow, moodily sucking the tube, while the young doctor, watch in hand, felt his pulse.

This was not the apartment Raffredo had

shown him (Finnerty had paid the grim landlady a week's rent in advance). It was a large
bare room, smelling vilely of carbolic acid;
besides his own cot there were four other beds,
occupied by four other men, — sick men, —
very sick men, apparently. At the end of five
minutes the doctor took out the thermometer
and read the temperature it registered.

"Where am I? Who are you? Why on
earth are you taking my temperature?" Finnerty demanded.

"*Zitto!*" said the man in white, laying a
finger on his lip. He next applied a stetho-
scope to Finnerty's heart, lungs, and abdomen.
The examination complete, an older man, also
in white, who had been attending to the person
in the next bed, joined them. There was a
discussion, with few words and many gestures.

"Signore," said the elder doctor in laborious
English, "there has been a mistake. Last
night, according to this record," he pointed to
a chart at the head of the bed, "you were
seized with violent convulsions in the Piazza
San Marco. The police 'called us up,' an

ambulance was sent, you were brought to the hospital. This morning I find you apparently perfectly well."

" So I am. The police are fools ! "

" *A chi lo dice ?* A misapprehension, yes, but how did it happen, I ask you ? "

" I remember something about it — the fact is, I was not quite myself."

" You were drunk ? "

" If you choose to call it that."

" What else, *caro ragazzo ?* " (dear boy).

" The police, *imbecili stupidi*, mistook *ubbriachezza* " (intoxication), " for — for illness, serious illness."

" Well, it's over now, except for a little headache."

" Not quite over. *Ebbene*, get up now and dress. When you have had breakfast we will see what can be done."

" Thank you. Don't trouble yourself about breakfast. I shall be better for a little walk before eating anything."

"Ah, *figlio mio*, that is the difficulty ! You may not take that little walk."

SAVONAROLA FINNERTY

" What do you mean ? "

" This is the cholera ward. You have been exposed to infection — *non abbia paura* " (do not fear) ; " you are in no more danger than ourselves or the nurses."

The man in the bed at Finnerty's right lay so still that he might be dead. His neighbor on the other side — a writhing figure, a tortured face — moaned aloud, —

" *Acqua, per l' amore della Madonna, una goccia d'acqua!* " (for the Madonna's sake, a drop of water).

III

" Still in Venice, Mr. Finnerty ? I supposed you 'd left," exclaimed de Ruyter Ruby. He was at work pasting clippings from the Venetian newspapers into a scrap-book. " I 'll be at liberty directly. The press over here say queer things about us over there."

" I bet I can tell you queerer things. How would this sound ? 'An American citizen seized in the public streets of Venice, put to sleep in a cholera ward with four cholera patients. Quarantined for three weeks in a beastly lazaretto !' "

Mr. Ruby hastily edged away. " What *do* you mean ? " he cried.

" That 's exactly what 's happened to me. You need n't be afraid. I 've been fumigated and steamed. I 'm an immune."

" What a dreadful thing ! How did it occur ? "

Finnerty told what he could remember of

125

his performance in the Piazza San Marco. "That mint-julep came rather high, did n't it?" he said. "I went to my lodgings this morning. They were let to a German, a fat man with spectacles! The landlady had ransacked my trunk and taken every cent she found. Gave me a receipted bill for the amount, made me pay three weeks' rent, though I heard she only waited twenty-four hours before re-letting the rooms. I 'm stranded high and dry, without a dollar. 'Still in Venice?' Unless you lend me money enough to get back to Rome I 'm likely to pass the rest of my life here at the public charge."

"Of course you shall have the money. Will two hundred francs do? I am rather short —"

"I shall take the four o'clock train for Rome — that is, if there 's nothing I can do to get even with the hospital people?"

"Well, I don't see — they were in their rights, don't you know? You had been exposed to infection —"

"Nor the landlady?"

"I can't advise trying. Lawsuits are endless things — it would cost more than it would come to."

"Then I'm off. Rome's comparatively a free country. I'll send you back the money as soon as I arrive."

At the railroad station a greasy interpreter pounced upon Finnerty.

"Sall I 'elp you, sare? Gif me ze bag."

"No, thank you. I can manage by myself."

"Buy ze ticket, weigh ze trunk, find ze lonely carriage?"

Finnerty flung impatiently away from the tormentor. At the ticket-office he placed his bag on the floor for a moment; the interpreter snatched it up.

"First-class ticket for Rome, straight through," said Finnerty, laying down one of Ruby's crisp new notes.

"*Roma, prima classe,*" the interpreter translated.

"That man understands English as well as you do," snapped Finnerty, counting his change (it was correct) and recovering his bag. Next

came the tiresome business of weighing his
trunk and paying for its transportation.   He
tipped the porter and the baggage weigher
generously.   The interpreter took heart.   The
game was worth the stalking.   The luggage
clerk wrote the *scontrino* (receipt) and handed
it to Finnerty, who made out that eight francs
were due on his trunk.   He gave the clerk a ten-
franc bill.   The official, after looking at it carefully, returned it with a polite bow.

" *Questo non è buono, si"or,*" he said.

" What ?   Not   enough ? "   Finnerty   demanded.

It was the interpreter's moment.

" He say ze money no good," he explained.

" If it 's good enough for them to give me,
it 's good enough for them to take.   Tell him
the man in the ticket-office gave me that bill."

The receipt and the ten-franc bill became
the storm centre of a whirlwind of talk.
Two impassive carabinieri, in long black coats
and cocked hats, joined the windy battle.
Finnerty heard " *ladri* " (thieves), one of the
few Italian words he knew, repeated many

times. It wanted only twenty minutes of four o'clock.

"Where's the station master?" Finnerty demanded.

"Littla *pazienza*, sare!" the interpreter implored.

A girl in gray walked by, followed by a porter carrying a bandbox and a cage with two white pigeons; she gave Finnerty a look of pity,—it was the Venus of the doves! Was she going by that train?

"Where *is* the station master?" Finnerty repeated.

"*Va bene, andiamo al capo!*" urged the interpreter. The whole party marched to the office of ultimate appeal, — in reality a police station, though Finnerty did not know this, — where a splendid official in uniform sat in judgment at a long table littered with papers. The interpreter, hat in hand, told Finnerty's story to the *capo,* who — stern, tired, perspiring profusely — listened with indifference. Finnerty heard the word "*ladri*" again and again. It was nearly four o'clock.

TWO IN ITALY

"*Ladri!* yes!" he cried; "you 're all thieves! All Italians from the King down are thieves and liars!"

"*Levate vi il cappello*," ordered the *capo* angrily.

"He say please take off ze hat," murmured the interpreter.

"No, I won't; they 've got theirs on."

"Ze *ufficiali* nevair remove ze hat," the interpreter explained.

"I 'm as good as they are!" Finnerty raged.

"*Allora levateglielo, voi*" (then take it off, you), the *capo* commanded in a terrible voice, pointing to the larger gendarme. The man drew his sword, and gave the brim of Finnerty's hat a clip that sent the big sombrero flying. It fell on the dirty floor.

"Take that!" yelled Finnerty, and struck the guard full in the face. In the ensuing scuffle both men fell to the ground. When Finnerty was kicked and pulled to his feet, he was handcuffed. The gendarme lay motionless. The clock struck four, the bell rang, the engine panted, the train steamed out of the

130

station. Through the haze of passion Finnerty saw a girl's face at the window of a third-class carriage looking at him compassionately. The interpreter picked up the sombrero, straightened the peacock feather, and put the hat on the prisoner's head.

"Ah, sare, a littla *pazienza*, only a littla *pazienza!* Now you go to ze prison for *lèse majesté* (ze *capo* he understand ze English); you may call *noi altri*" (we others) "*ladri*, but not ze King, no."

Finnerty was marched to the police gondola. On that dismal journey to the jail, his face pressed close to the small grating at the back of the boat, he saw a friend.

"Hi! Raffredo! Gondolier!" he cried desperately.

Raffredo, explaining the glories of the Royal Garden to his fare — the spectacled German who had taken Finnerty's lodging — did not hear the hail. As the big black prison gondola passed him, Raffredo was half conscious of a familiar face behind the bars. With the next sweep of the oars the prison

131

boat glided around a corner, passed under the Ponte dei Sospiri (the Bridge of Sighs), and stopped at the door of the *carceri criminali* (criminal prison).

* * * * * * *

" Who 's Savonarola Finnerty, Esq.? " asked the consul, a spare energetic Yankee.

" An American artist who was in Venice while you were away," de Ruyter Ruby explained.

" Here 's a letter to him in your hand-writing, returned from Rome."

" Hullo ! That 's odd ! I wrote asking him to send back the money I lent him to get there."

" You 'll never see it again."

" He 's not that sort. Finnerty 's straight — but he is queer. I don't quite like his not having reached Rome."

" Has he any friends there ? "

" Plenty, I should say. He spoke of knowing Patsy."

" Then wire for news of him."

The answer to the telegram was received

before night: " Finnerty missing. Find him. Chalk it up to Patsy."

" That's definite," said the consul, who had great respect for Patsy. " We must see what's become of Finnerty. Now, young man, you have just forty-eight hours to prove to me that you're worth your keep." The consul had returned unexpectedly from his well-earned holiday. He was not exactly pleased with the state of things he found at the consulate.

Ruby first sought the *capo stazione.* The man had been on duty only a week.

" There are so many strangers at this season," he said, " it is not possible to remember the gentleman you describe. Inquiries shall be made. I will let the Signor Consolo know, be assured, if I find any trace of him."

The ticket-seller, naturally, had no recollection of a man who, but for the intervention of Heaven, might have cost him his post. The office of the luggage clerk was closed, the interpreter was at luncheon — it appeared that nobody had ever seen Finnerty.

133

Outside the station Ruby paused, uncertain as to the next move in the game. Twirling alternately his little mustache and his two-headed cane, he looked for counsel up to the pitiless sky (it was high noon of a scorching day in early September) and down into the canal. The sunlight glinted on the polished *ferro* of a neat gondola — flashed from the teeth and eyes of a handsome gondolier lounging against the *felze*. Ruby hailed him.

"*Poppe!* Do you remember that signorino with the green coat and the peacock feather you brought to the consulate?"

"*Per Baccho!* I remember him well, *si'or;* un bel giovanotto, ma molto originale!* He engaged me for a week. I went to his lodging every morning for seven days, but he had evidently left Venice."

"He has disappeared," said Ruby, "but I do not think he has left Venice. Help me find him, and there will be a *buona mano* of fifty francs for you."

"We will find him. Not for the money, *si'or*, but because he was *tanto buono, tanto bello!* Why, he paid me for a week in advance, fearing, I suppose, to lose his money."

"You are quite sure you have seen nothing of him ?"

"Wait. One afternoon, — *corpo!* it must be fifteen days since, — as the prison gondola passed I saw a man behind the grate who looked like him — but it is not possible — no ! "

As there was no other, Ruby followed the clew Raffredo offered. It led to the *carceri criminali,* where a prisoner corresponding to Finnerty was awaiting trial for *lèse majesté* and assault and battery on one of the King's guard. For two days and nights Ruby worked harder than he had ever worked in his life. Within the time limit set by his chief, he succeeded in obtaining an order for the prisoner's release.

"Yes, this is the gentleman I am looking for," said Mr. Ruby, as the jailer unlocked the door of number four, a small stifling cell. Two perfectly naked men (the heat was intense) sat at a table playing dominos. The whitewashed walls were covered with bold charcoal sketches of the players, disputing, wrestling, casting the dice. The elder face was sinister; the younger, weak. A third man in a yellow shirt, and a pair of creased breeches hanging loose below the knee, lay asleep on a bare board, his coat folded under his head for a pillow. At that moment an attendant set down on the table—knocking over the dominos as he did so—a large bowl of plain boiled macaroni, three wedges of coarse bread, and a pitcher of water.

"*Poverino!*" whispered Raffredo; "observe, Sir Consul, how thin he has grown. *Magari!* It is not wonderful,—macaroni without *parmigiano* or even tomato sauce, and *water!* Diàscoci!*"

Ruby touched the sleeper on the arm.

"Finnerty, old chap! Wake up! It's all right."

Savonarola, dazed, gaunt, unshaven, sat up and looked uncertainly at the deliverers. Raffredo burst into tears, knelt beside him and petted him like a child.

"*E trovato! Coraggio, caro si̇̈or! Tanto*

giovine, tanto bello." (He is found! Courage, dear gentleman! So young, so handsome.)

"Did I kill that guard? Am I to be hanged or electrocuted? What are they going to do with me?"

"Give you a bath, a dinner, a mint-julep, if you like. First of all, get you out of this."

"You mean it? It's really *you*, Ruby? This *is* Raffredo?"

"Brace up, old man, you're free! I've fixed it up, paid a big fine — here's your discharge."

Finnerty stood up, spread out his arms, and drew a long breath. His clouded eyes were clearing fast. "Have you any tobacco with you?" he asked.

Ruby gave him a new box of cigarettes.

"Here, you fellows, share and share alike." He put half the cigarettes in the hand of each domino player (they were already busy gobbling the macaroni). "If you did murder a magistrate, Nino — that's what he's accused of — I am sure he deserved it. I hope you'll get out soon and kill another."

137

The elder of the players nodded his thanks and went on with his meal.

"Good-bye, Obadia, forgery's not the worst crime!" Finnerty shook hands with the two men; then, to Ruby, "Come! let's get out of this!"

* * * * * * *

"Ai, Patsy! Where art thou?" cried Attilio.

"Coo ar-r-r-ra coo, ar-r-r-ra coo!" came from a wicker bird-cage (hanging against the rose-covered wall of Patsy's garden), where two white doves with pink feet cooed and cooed to each other all day long. The brown and white puppy scrambled delightedly over Attilio.

"I am a little early," said Attilio; "the others will be here soon."

It was the usual hour of meeting. Attilio lighted a cigarette and played with the dog. He had not long to wait before the gate opened, and Patsy, with Finnerty behind him, entered. Pietro followed with the luggage.

"Well returned, *caro* Savo'," cried Attilio. "What a surprise, what a pleasure to see thee again! Didst thou enjoy Venice?"

The Tiber

SAVONAROLA FINNERTY

"Well, I spent one night in a cholera hospital, three weeks in quarantine, fifteen days in prison, if you call that enjoyment."

"Oh, unfortunate! Oh, poor one! Thou makest me rage. Did I not warn thee against the Venetians?"

"You did. I passed the last night at the consul's — crusty old boy, but all right. After I was in bed he or his nephew (a queer duck) locked my door on the outside. That didn't keep me awake! They gave me the breakfast of my life: fishballs and buckwheat cakes. They took me to the station in the consul's gondola, and put me on the train. They must have tipped the guard; he pestered me with attentions all the way to Rome. Think of their telegraphing you to meet me, Patsy!"

"The consul doesn't know that you're only *half* mad, Savo'," laughed Patsy.

"Rome's good enough for me. As to the Venetians, may they — "

Finnerty's story was told and retold many times. He and Attilio said such damaging things about the Venetians that Patsy — al-

139

ways on the side of the absent — grew restive ; his patience was worn out.

" Hold up, old man," he said at last; " how about Savo' Finnerty, — his thirst that got him into quarantine, his temper that put him in quod ? "

Finnerty changed the subject.

" Hullo ! where did those fowls come from ? " He pointed to the wicker cage.

" They belong to a lady.   I 'm keeping them till she finds her apartment."

" Brown eyes, yellow hair, looks like an American ? "

" That describes Miss Fair."

The Venus of the doves was in Rome.

VI

SAVONAROLA FINNERTY

(WHAT I KNEW OF HIM)

CHAPTER VI

SAVONAROLA FINNERTY
(WHAT I KNEW OF HIM)

I

THE BÁLIA'S BATH

"ROSA says she will not take a bath," Pompilia announced.

"Make her! There are enough of you women, without my help, I suppose?" said the great doctor. He has the face of an archangel and the obstinacy of a mule.

"'*Scusi*,' she says, 'for a nursing woman to take a bath means death.' *Poverina*, she is very ignorant," murmured Pompilia.

"Would you mind trying?" asked the doctor, looking at me.

"You must," cried Patsy. "Hear the little beggar cursing the hour he saw the light! He's hungry. We must not let him starve to death, after all the trouble we've had to get him safely born!"

143

TWO IN ITALY

I found Rosa in an immense room, half bar-rack, half prison. It was paved with brick, had a stone roof and walls, and eight high windows. A long tin bathtub, with a linen sheet under the water (the tub was hired for the occasion), stood near a brazier filled with burning char-coal. On a low chair sat Nena, a little gnarled old woman, with a neatly swaddled infant on her knees.

> "*Io vorrei andar in carrozzella per andare, per andare nella luna,*
> *Per vedere la piu bella delle donne, delle donne de lassù !*"
> (I should like to drive in a little carriage, to go, to go, to the moon ;
> To see the most beautiful of the women up there !)

She crooned to the new-born, whimpering in her arms.

Rosa stood in a corner, her back to the wall, sullen and angry.

"No, *no*, I tell you ! " she stormed. "I did not come here to be murdered, but to give milk to that *povero bambino*" (poor baby). "Let the accursed *vecchierella* nurse him if she can ! "

144

"See, Rosa, the water is quite warm; it cannot hurt you. Look at the pretty coral neck-
lace the master bought you, and the beautiful
cap. Who ever saw such splendid scarlet ribbons? How they will become you!" coaxed
Pompilia.

Rosa, a black-browed woman from Subiaco
in the Sabine Hills, showed her white teeth;
drew from the busk of her corset (worn outside the linen shirt) a thin sharp dagger with
a handle of two enlaced hearts, and stood at
bay.

"I can do nothing with Rosa," I said to the
three men waiting in the salon. "Go for Dr.
Vernon. I believe she could manage her."

She did. Somehow that small plain English
girl — a practising physician in the slums of
Whitechapel, come to Rome for a month's
vacation — coaxed, cajoled, or cowed the big
black *bália* into submitting to the very necessary ceremony of a bath before the little atom
of humanity was committed to her broad brown
breast.

"It's all right now, Mr. Finnerty," said Dr.

10 145

Vernon. "I 've scrubbed Rosa from top to toe (she needed it). What a splendid savage! The great doctor has turned your wife and the little fellow over to me. Don't be afraid to trust me. I 've been doing this sort of thing for five years. Run away now like a good man; this is no place for a husband. Won't you please take him home to dinner?"

"He looks as if he had n't eaten a square meal for a month," whispered Patsy.

"How can I, when you have commandeered all my women for service here?"

"Oh, have a *fritto misto* and *du' spaghetti* sent up from the *trattoria*. I 'll wait on table. It 's not worth while doing things by halves!" So perforce I took them both home and fed them.

When the Finnerty baby was six months old, the young mother sent for me. Dr. Vernon had gone back to her London slums. In her absence the little wind-flower of a woman turned to the great doctor and to me.

"Rosa stabbed Angelo in the stomach last night," Mrs. Finnerty quavered, "because he said she stole the sugar. Can I keep such a volcano in the house?"

"Let's see the baby," said the doctor.

Rosa, splendid in her *bália* finery, brought in the child and proudly exhibited his fat, creased legs and arms.

"*Povero Checco!*" she sang. "What a poor little *miserabile* thou wast when I took thee! Who gave thee all this good flesh? Rosa, the thief!"

The wind-flower shook as she held out her thin arms for the child.

"Not yet, *mamma mia*, if you please, not till I have had my dinner; then send Rosa into the kitchen to clean the pots!" raged the savage Sabine.

"Rosa's right, Mrs. Finnerty. You can't let her go with the hot weather coming on. She's the finest wet-nurse in Rome; make the best of her."

"She is half whirlwind, half virago," the baby's mother lamented.

"So! She can't entertain your company in the salon, and she can't play the piano, but

147

she's a good wet-nurse, eh? Lock up the sugar, dock her coffee and wine every time she gets into a passion, and put up with her tantrums." Leaving us to consider this excellent advice, the great doctor departed to visit a royal personage. He has but two classes of patients, — the mighty, who pay him immense fees, and the meek, who pay him nothing. He is quite as faithful to one as to the other.

"You will wait and have tea with us?" Mrs. Finnerty invited. "I will call Savonarola. He is in the studio."

Finnerty, after his son's birth, had given his wife, as an appropriate present, a life-sized cast of the Psyche in the Naples Museum. Angelo, the old servant who took care of those three babes in the nest, coming in with the tea-tray, found me standing before the copy of that sublime fragment of classic sculpture.

"You admire that statue, Signora?" he asked.

"I admire it very greatly, Angelo; do not you?"

" Ah ! you should have seen it before it was broken ; it was a *capo d' opera* — one of the most to be admired works of the Signore Finneté. What a pity it got so badly smashed ! "

Pupils had been found for Finnerty. The big barrack of a room where I first saw Rosa was now a studio. Here every morning four American and two English ladies made dreadful caricatures in clay of Rosa and the baby, of Mrs. Finnerty, and, when he could be spared, of Angelo.

" It is rather inconvenient," Mrs. Finnerty confessed, " but it saves hiring models ; they are so expensive. Yesterday Savo' asked that old beggar who sits in the Corso selling matches to pose for him. What do you think he said ? "

" You must not mind what such people say. You want him to pose, not to talk. He is the handsomest old man in Rome."

" That 's why Savo' wants him. He looked at us quite scornfully and said, ' *Grazie ;* it would not be worth my while to come for

less than ten francs a day.' Think of it, a
beggar!"

"But what a beggar! Mr. Finnerty is
right; he's worth any price."

"That old rascal in the Corso?" said Finnerty, who had just come in. "I must look
farther even if I fare worse. I shall need a
model for a long time, and I must get him
cheap. My 'next' will be a composition of
colossal size."

"What is the subject?" I asked.

"The Oversoul before the creation of the
world, brooding over the universe."

"Think what it will cost to put the Oversoul
into plaster," I said to Patsy the next time we
talked about the Finnertys, as we did very
often that winter. "I suppose it's safe not to
go farther than plaster?"

"Perfectly safe," Patsy agreed. "Savo's
serious compositions never go beyond plaster.
If he would only stick to animals! Nobody
can touch him there, but he thinks them be-
neath him."

"You might let Savo' know," said J., "that I

have found a model for him. He can get him cheap, — his food, tobacco, and a couple of francs a day will satisfy the chap."

" Where did you find him ? " I asked.

" On the steps of the Piazza di Spagna (time out of mind the models' exchange) of course."

" At two francs a day ? No, seriously ? "

" That evening I walked home from Albano, the night of the full moon," said J., " I saw a fire on the Campagna, only a little way from the road, in front of a *capanna* — you know, one of those reed huts the shepherds build for shelter against sun and storm. I was cold and tired. The blaze looked comforting. I started for it. A fierce white sheep dog sprang at me, growling. At that a man in a slouch hat with a long cloak — he was a *pecorajo* " (shepherd) " got up from the ground by the fire and threw a stone and a curse at that wolfish beast.

" '*Chette possino scannà!*' he said to his dog ; to me, '*favorisca*,' and made me free of the fire, — all the comfort the poor devil had. As we sat over the few burning brands, in the broad moonlight, among the ghosts of last year's thistles, talking about sheep, the *pecorajo* began to yawn. Such prodigious yawning I never saw. He looked as sleepy as I felt. I turned my back to the fire and stretched myself along the ground. I must have fallen asleep, for the next thing I knew the *pecorajo* was shaking me by the arm. ' *Qui meno si dorme, meglio est !* ' he said. I must have been dreaming, for it seemed to me that one of the ancient Romans was speaking to me ; certainly that was the nearest thing to Latin I ever heard an Italian say."

"That fellow probably saved you from the *perniciosa*. Sleeping on the Campagna is a pretty sure way to malarial fever," said Patsy.

"I suppose it is. The *pecorajo* himself (his name is Tommaso) has a touch of malaria ; he 's in need of a little treatment. You 'll ask the doctor to look out for him ? "

"We have asked the doctor to look out for so many people — " I said.

"What 's the difference ? When the doctors want to learn things, they experiment on those poor peasants. It 's their business to

The Yawning Shepherd

take care of them when they are ill," cried Patsy.

" I gave the *pecorajo* the address of my studio, and said I could give him a place to sleep," J. confessed.

" If he should appear," I temporized.

" He was sitting on the steps when I went to the studio this morning. I left him asleep in the straw of an empty stall in the stable under the studio. The best bed, he told me, he had slept in for a long time."

The doctor took J.'s point of view and adopted the shepherd as a patient. Finnerty fell in love with him, and engaged him as a model; another *pecorajo* now minds the sheep. Thus was Tommaso added to our circle.

Finnerty's new studio was in the ruins of the Thermæ of Diocletian: a mighty red brick skeleton, all that remains of a once stupendous marble chamber — the tepidarium perhaps — of Rome's greatest bath. Here he set up the colossal statue of the Oversoul. He threw himself into his work with incredible energy. The mammoth figure grew astonishingly quickly. The Oversoul was a huge winged figure seated in the Occidental attitude on a fragment of cloud. With the exception of the pose, the spirit of the thing was Oriental, suggesting the conventional representations of Buddha. The face was contemplative, the eyes downcast, the hands folded. In size it was to be only smaller than the singing statue of Memnon at Luxor, on the Nile. Its immediate destination was the White City by the Lake, — then still a dream, now a glorious memory. In those long summer days, the artists' harvest season, Savo' worked from daylight to dark.

" It 's terrific to see him," I said to Patsy. " Can flesh and blood stand such a labor of Hercules ? "

" He can't keep it up long," said Patsy. " Now his strength is as the strength of ten, because he is a little mad. Did you notice that fanatical gleam in his eyes ? "

" And the statue ? "

" Quite mad. He 'll see it himself some day. There 's no doubt about Savo's imagina-

tion; the question is about his character. Time
alone shows that. I am not quite sure whether
Savo' is a great artist or only a great dreamer."

Savo' said it helped him to have us watch
him work, so I often dropped into the studio
with J., or Patsy, or both at the end of the
day. One evening we found him seated on the
staging in his blue cotton sculptor's blouse,
smoking a cigarette. For once he was idle;
sitting inert and weary, leaning against one
mighty wing of his Colossus.

" How have you been getting on ? " asked
Patsy.

" As you see. Sometimes I think it cannot
be done in time for the opening of the World's
Fair," Savo' sighed.

" What then ? "

" Then I shall put it up myself, somewhere
outside the grounds by the edge of the Lake,
where everybody can see it."

" If you want to make money, put it on
piles in the Lake, and let boats for people to
row out and see it. Make it a side show, at a
quarter a head," said J.

"Who laughs last laughs best," said Savo' quietly, blowing out white rings of smoke that ascended like incense to the downcast face of the brooding Colossus. The man's eyes were clouded, his broad shoulders were bent; even his mop of chestnut hair (it usually stood straight on end), matted with perspiration, lay damp and lifeless on his forehead.

"Savo's at the end of this stunt," said Patsy, as we went away. "I must take him away with me for a trip."

"He can't afford —" I began.

"That doesn't matter," said Patsy; "somebody else can afford."

"Who is paying for the Oversoul?" I asked.

"One of his scholars; a rich woman with a bigger income than she can spend. I never saw anything so refreshing as Savo's indifference to money."

"Isn't it rather inconvenient to his friends sometimes?" I timidly suggested.

"There you go, like the rest. It's the taint of trade. We Americans can't get rid of it, try ever so hard! There's no offence in Savo's views because there's no pose. When he was in Paris (we were in the same atelier), Savo' had a good allowance from a fat richling who was backing him. His money came 'fresh and fresh' the first of every month. For the first fifteen days of the month Finnerty dined at the Café Foyau, for the next ten days at Clarisse's, the last week anywhere. I went with him once to a place in a cellar kept by an old witch. She had a great '*pot au feu*,' a caldron full of stew, boiling over a fire. You paid a sou ; the witch gave you a three-tined steel fork, and you speared what you could from her caldron. At my first try I split a potato and got nothing but the crack. Savo' was a 'dab' at the game ; he drew the prize, — a bone with a whole hock of mutton. As long as his money lasted, Savo' shared it with whoever was hard up ; now that he has a wife and child, is n't it our business to stand by him ? "

II

FINNERTY refused to take the trip Patsy
offered him; he could not leave the Oversoul.
The vast creature of his fancy threatened, like
a second Frankenstein's monster, to crush the
life out of its creator. Finnerty's patroness,
falling out of conceit with him and his *magnum
opus*, withdrew her support. Somehow, in
spite of this, the wonderful great statue got
finished, packed, and shipped to America.
Then came the dire news that the Colossus had
been broken in transportation, and was held at
New York for freight charges. At this Finnerty fell into a state of nervous melancholia,
verging on madness. Patsy Puss-in-Boots,
Finnerty's good genius, was at his wits' end
how to help him.

"Do you know," he said, "I don't like to
look into Finnerty's eyes now."

"His little wife is poorly too. Her skin
was as smooth as Martin's" (the baby had been

given his father's name in full) "when they
were married; now she has crow's-feet — at
her age!"

"*And* a husband and a baby!

> Time, like a fishwife, does n't fight fair;
> He scratches your face and pulls out your hair,"

said Patsy, consolingly. "All we can do is to
'goody them up,' and keep a weather-eye open
for windfalls."

We were waiting for Mrs. Finnerty, who
presently appeared with Martin Luther, a
magnificent child, in her arms. Rosa had
gone back to Subiaco. Angelo now discharged
the duties of nurse, cook, and *cameriére*.

"Is n't Martin too heavy for you to carry,
Mrs. Finnerty?" I asked.

"Oh, no. Angelo will take him as soon as
he has brought our tea. He worships baby,
but he has such strange ways! Last night
Savo' and I dined at Bucci's (I thought it
might cheer him up). When we came home,
it must have been past ten o'clock, the house
was empty. Savo' rushed over to the *osteria*

opposite. There sat Angelo at a table drinking among a lot of coachmen, with Martin in his arms. He said he had business there, and thought it was better to take baby with him than to leave him at home alone."

"What is Angelo's business, besides taking care of you?" asked Patsy.

"He is a seer — a dreamer. I had forgotten it was Thursday, Angelo's busy day. The lottery is drawn on Friday; some of the people in the neighborhood pay Angelo for giving them lucky numbers. He has been fortunate lately; last week Giggi della Fiumaccia won five hundred francs on a number Angelo gave him."

"There is a strange gentleman outside asking for the Signore," Angelo announced, giving Mrs. Finnerty a card. She read the name aloud:

DE RUYTER RUBY
DENTISTE
(*Ancien Diplomate*)
12 A Via Frattina

"Do you know him?" she appealed to Patsy.
"Oh, yes, Ruby's an old friend of your

husband's and mine. Let him come in. I 'll introduce him. Savo' will be back soon."

The *ancien diplomate* bustled into the bare little salon, where, after five minutes, he was as much at home as Patsy himself.

"Nice place you 've got here, Mrs. Finnerty," he said. "Those doves remind me of Venice. You are fond of animals?"

"The doves came from Venice; both my husband and I *have* to have animals. Tommaso (he 's the model) has given Savo' the loveliest little cosset lamb from the flock of sheep he used to tend. The lamb lives at the studio. He is as tame as a kitten. Baby loves him."

"You have left Venice, Ruby? Given up diplomacy?" asked Patsy.

"For the moment. My uncle lost his place when the administration changed."

"So you 've come to Rome and put up your shingle as a dentist. Where did you learn that trade?"

"I am a graduate of the Boisé City Dental College. Until I receive a diplomatic appointment —"

SAVONAROLA FINNERTY

"You've returned to your first love? Good enough!"

"I hope Mr. Finnerty is doing well? Lots of orders and that sort of thing?" Ruby asked politely.

Mrs. Finnerty changed color and hesitated.

"Famously," Patsy assured him; "he's overwhelmed with work. That's the way with our people; we either let an artist starve to death or we kill him with orders."

"There's a rich man called Ghost here — funny name, isn't it? He's very sensitive about it — who has brought me a letter of introduction from my uncle. He's interested in art, wants to see studios and that sort of thing," said Mr. Ruby.

Patsy gave me a warning look; the fish must be left to his angling.

"I'm not in that line myself," Ruby went on. "I have no time to go round with him; besides, I am a stranger in Rome. I have my practice to work up. I thought perhaps Mr. Finnerty might—"

"No, no," interrupted Patsy. "Savo's time

is too precious. Bring your friend to my place, Via Flaminia outside the Porta del Popolo — all the cabmen know it. I will show him every studio in Rome worth seeing."

The *ancien diplomate* burbled with joy. "I say, you're awfully kind. People come over here for a vacation and expect us fellows who have our living to make — hard enough job in Italy anyway — to devote all our time to going 'sight-seeing' with them."

"Oh, that's part of 'the price of Europe.' It's a long price, whatever way you look at it," sighed Patsy.

We heard nothing of Patsy for a fortnight; that meant he was playing the fish, probably with a chance of landing it. Then we received a summons, begging us to come to Finnerty's studio that afternoon to meet Mr. Ghost of Boisé City. We arrived a few moments before the appointed time. Finnerty was alone. He looked better; his eyes were no longer desperate, only depressed. In the middle of the studio, so tragically empty since the departure of the Colossus, stood some composition in clay wrapped in wet cloths.

"You 're at work again?" cried J.

Finnerty took off the covering and showed a portrait bust of a fat man with mutton-chop whiskers.

"Do you call that *work?* It 's nothing but an infernal pot-boiler!"

Finnerty felt the gray clay, found it too dry, filled a syringe with water, and sprinkled the bust.

"Nonsense!" said J. He shut one eye and "squinted" at the portrait. "It 's ripping good stuff, and you know it."

"I am sure it 's an excellent likeness," I said. "Why, the thing *speaks!* "

"I think it is like Ghost, though why he, or anybody else, should want it— Here he is now; you can judge of the likeness yourself."

Mr. Ghost — a gentleman of benevolent aspect, a trifle fatter than the bust — came hurriedly into the studio. Though he shook hands politely with us, he had eyes only for

165

Finnerty. He was evidently fascinated by this (to him) new species of man.

"How do you like the marble, Mr. Finnerty? It's a magnificent piece of Carrara, your friend Patsy tells me; there's not a flaw in it." He passed his beringed hands caressingly over a large block of white marble that stood in a corner of the studio.

" Oh, it's all right," said Finnerty, moodily, "if I only knew what to do with it."

" You'll see the figure wrestling to get out of the stone, as Michael Angelo did, some day, Mr. Finnerty. Trust to your inspiration, sir !"

" Inspiration ?" cried Finnerty; "inspiration means perspiration! 'Wrestling'? When I think how I have wrestled with that Over-soul — "

" It's uncommonly good marble, I should say," J. hastily interrupted.

Finnerty nodded gloomily.

"I bought it cheap, at the sale of that French sculptor's effects the other day," Mr. Ghost explained. " I am building a house. It will be the largest private residence west of Chicago.

SAVONAROLA FINNERTY

Mr. Finnerty has promised to make me an original composition for my new art gallery."

"Patsy promised," Finnerty amended (I could have boxed his disconsolate ears). "There he is now; ask him what *he* sees in the marble."

Mrs. Finnerty with Martin, followed by the pet lamb, and convoyed by Patsy (light, and tireless of foot as Mercury, messenger of the gods), appeared in the flood of sunlight the opened door let into the grim studio.

"This is my wife," said Finnerty.

"I am so pleased to meet you, Mr. Corpse," said Mrs. Finnerty.

"Ghost, marm. The name was originally Geist," corrected its owner. "It was changed by act of legislature."

Patsy looked murder at the poor little woman, who held up Martin as if to screen herself behind the child. Finnerty laughed openly at his wife. As she stood there, shy, lovely, blushing, the baby in her arms, the pet lamb snuggling at her feet, Finnerty's dull, indifferent eyes fastened upon her, took fire and depth, positively glowed with inner light.

" Stand beside the marble, hold the boy as you did just now — God! she's just the right size. How would that subject do for your art gallery, Mr. Ghost?" With a bit of charcoal Finnerty rapidly sketched the group on the face of the marble block.

" It's the best subject in the world, Mr. Finnerty! Do it, sir, at your own price, and I'll settle the bills."

" Goo!" babbled Martin Luther. Pleased by Mr. Ghost's cable of gold watch-chain and his glistening scarf-pin, the baby stretched his arms towards the gentleman from Boisé City.

" Children always like me," said Ghost; "may I relieve you, marm?"

VII

THE HERMIT OF PIETRO ANZIERI

CHAPTER VII

THE HERMIT OF PIETRO ANZIERI

I

THE MIRACULOUS PICTURE

THE rivalry between Roccaraso and Pescocostanzo dates from the earliest settlement of these two Abruzzi villages in the fifth century. The hermit of Pietro Anzieri knows something of local tradition. He will tell you — if you can have patience with his slow, halting speech, his funny, fumbling manner — old tales of the old feud. He had been repeating to his niece Carolina a terrible story of ravishment; how on a certain May morning twenty of the girls and women of Roccaraso, bleaching their linen in the meadow outside the walled town, were surprised and carried off by the men of Pescocostanzo. When the Roccarasans returned from the expedition that had left their wives

171

and daughters unprotected, they wreaked a prompt and bloody vengeance. Both kidnapping and chastisement occurred in the thirteenth century. The old unkindness still lives on; it echoes in the hermit's talk, in his distrust of all that comes out of Pescocostanzo.

"*Ma che!* All that happened so many years ago, do let us forget about it!" exclaimed Carolina, who had heard the story fifty times. "They were very bad people, were they not?"

"Bad?" squeaked the hermit. "Bad? They were monsters!"

"Then," argued Carolina, with charming reasonableness, — "then, *zio mio*, let us not think of them more." Carolina had no patience with historians who perpetuate the memory of bad people or wicked actions.

"That was not the beginning," grumbled the hermit; "when the founders of Roccaraso, driven from the plains by the Saracens, took refuge with their women and children in these great mountains (where *il buon Dio* meant there to be room for all), how did the accursed Pescocostanzans treat those poor unfortunate

172

fugitives? Answer me that! Even the children know that story!"

Carolina laughed, good-humoredly repeating, "*Non pensiamoci piu!* Why should we remember those bad people? Is it not more meritorious to remember the blessed saints? Look now at what I have brought you! Last night grandfather's black-faced sheep took it into her stupid head to fall into the stone quarry and get killed. This morning every bit of her flesh was sold; the Sindaco bought one hind-quarter, the Parroco the other. Yes, we made a good thing out of it. I begged the neck of mutton from grandfather to make broth for my brother and you."

"Our Lady, whose poor servant I am, will reward Sor' Giacomo and you, too, *nipotina mia*. It is long since I have had the taste of meat; it appears to me that this mutton-broth will re-establish my strength."

The whitewashed hermitage stands high above a dazzling gray highroad near the valley of the Rasino. In the corridor adjoining the chapel, where the hermit and Carolina were

talking, six sleeping berths the length of a
man were fastened against the wall ; a skull
and crossbones hung above each bed. The
hermit opened the rough cupboard where he
kept his provisions, — a loaf of hard bread,
some corn meal, and a bottle of *acquavite.*
Carolina washed the cleanest bowl she could
find and set the broth away in the cupboard.

" Look now at what I have for Our Lady ! "
She produced a bouquet of pink paper roses.

"She will reward you.   Come into the chapel;
you yourself shall arrange the flowers."

The tiny chapel of the hermitage contains
one small altar, a pair of handsome candlesticks, and two lustre vases.   An old painting
of Madonna and Child — smoke-blackened
and badly out of repair — hangs over the
altar.   Carolina dusted the chapel and arranged
her flowers in the vases.

" You look better, uncle," she said cheerfully.   " Our Lady is not unmindful of you.
You will be yourself again in another week."

" All things are possible through Our Lady's
intervention.   You remember what happened

when the men of Pescocostanzo tried to steal
the holy picture? First they came with a carriage and four horses. Would you believe it,
that picture, which I can carry alone, grew to
so great a weight the horses could not move
the carriage! Then they came with six oxen
in an ox cart. Since that blessed night when
Our Lady lay in a stable, the ox has been less
stupid an animal than is commonly supposed.
Those oxen refused to stir a step with the holy
picture. At last wicked men, with hearts
harder than the dumb beasts', took it in their
arms and carried it away to their church in
Pescocostanzo. The next morning the picture
was back in its old place where you now see it,
having flown all the way by night."

"She has great powers, Romito" (hermit),
said Carolina, rising from her knees. "May
she grant the grace of my dear brother's
recovery!"

"How did you leave poor Giulio?" asked
the hermit, his lean, lank unshaven face, his
big foolish eyes grown tender with sympathy.

"*E tutto consumato!*" (consumed, wasted

175

away) "his cough is terrible." Her eyes brimmed over with tears.

"Despair not; above all, cease not to pray," said the hermit, earnestly. Just then the government doctor put his head into the chapel.

"Ah, Romito, there you are! I have brought your medicine. It will do you no good, however, if you *will* stay in this damp place when you have fever and ought to be in bed. Is that you, Carolina? How has your brother Giulio been sleeping?"

"He cannot sleep. He will not eat — not even those things of luxury you ordered for him. *Ahimé!* The money I have spent on white bread, fresh eggs, marsala wine for him!"

"Lost his appetite, eh? I must give him a tonic."

"I fear the winter will be very hard on him, *dottore mio;* what do you think?" she said timidly.

The doctor, looking down, flicked the dust from his high boots with his riding-whip.

Carolina read his face with keen, anguished eyes.

" He will die ? " she cried shrilly, facing for the first time the thing she had long feared.

The doctor murmured a perfunctory " *Mentre che se campa, c'é sempre speranza !* " (while there is life there is hope).

" *Caro dottore,* have patience. You remember the young officer who was *afflitissimo* with this same terrible malady ? To tell the truth, he looked worse than Giulio two years ago. You sent *him* to a far country. *He* is cured. Why not send my brother to that same place ? "

" Giulio is better off in his own home, with you to take care of him."

" *Scusi, caro dottore,* you are a wise, distinguished gentleman; I am only a poor ignorant girl, but I know that Giulio cannot live through another winter in Roccaraso. Could he live longer in that other country ? "

The doctor was silent.

" If I bring the money and put it in your hand, you will save my brother ? Though we are poor creatures, — hardly better than the beasts of the fields, — life is as sweet to us as to you gentlefolks."

She put her hand to her lips, then laid it on the skirts of his coat.

"The young officer is at Davos-Platz in Switzerland. That he is better there does not prove the climate would suit Giulio. Davos is very far from here, two days and nights in the train, perhaps even longer. You, poor child, cannot afford to send your brother to Switzerland. Besides —." He paused.

"What would the journey cost?"

"Perhaps two hundred francs."

"How much to keep him there?"

"He might live for three or four francs a day."

"*Madonna mia!* But that is robbery!"

"To travel one must have *soldi* in the pocket," said the doctor.

"And we others," put in the hermit, "have only the headache in the pocket."

"Look, Carolina," said the doctor, earnestly; "unless you stop worrying about Giulio, you

cannot be a good nurse to him ; a smile is
better than a plaster. All the same I will send
a tonic to help his appetite. Run away now
like a good child ; it is the Romito's turn to
talk about *his* aches and pains."

Carolina's eyes probed the doctor's, then
dropped humbly. She drew her kerchief close
about her face, hid a mouth fresh and young
as a half-opened flower, murmured a word of
farewell, and passed out into the sunlight.
The Romito's simple case was quickly dis-
posed of.

" While you have fever stay in bed and
fast ; when the fever leaves you keep out of
doors and eat all the good things Carolina
brings you."

" I do not say it because she is my dead
sister's child, but because it is the truth :
Carolina is a good, well-educated girl, a match
for any young fellow. She is an orphan, —
between us two, that is not a bad thing when
a man is looking for a wife, — she has a good
bit of money, at least four thousand francs.
Sor' Giacomo will leave all he has to her and

Giulio — you yourself know better than another how long the boy is likely to live to enjoy his share. She will have a bigger dowry than any girl in Roccaraso."

"Whom will she marry?" asked the doctor. He loved his people as the shepherds thereabouts love their sheep.

"She has hopes of Francesco the Sindaco's son, though nothing is settled. He has great pretensions and is very avaricious. My niece, too, is ambitious; she knows her worth and wishes to make a good marriage. That is proper and natural."

"She is the finest girl in ten villages," said the doctor. "I hope she will get a good husband."

"If you or your Signora said as much to the Sindaco?"

"Excuse me. I have not time to make marriages; besides, Carolina deserves a better husband."

The Romito stared. "She must go to Naples to make a better match," he said.

"Bah! Francesco is small, puny, rickety;

180

has a nasty temper too. There goes a man fit for Carolina, *Diamine!* What a couple they would make!"

The Romito limped to the chapel door and looked out. He saw a tall fellow swinging along the road.

"That is Roffredo Ferrari, nephew of old Ferrari who used to carry the mails from Pescocostanzo to Rivisondoli. When Roffredo was a boy the family moved to North America. The old uncle died last summer. Roffredo came back to settle the estate. It is not to be denied he is a handsome chap. A thousand pities he is of Pescocostanzo."

"See, he will overtake Carolina," said the doctor. "Are they acquainted?"

"Who knows? All young men and young women are acquainted through the eyes."

The doctor — he was still young — laughed.

"You have not forgotten the ways of the young, Romito."

"No wise man ever forgets them; when a pretty girl takes to coming to the chapel, nine times out of ten some lad remembers at about

the same time to say his prayers.   There is a
song my mother used to sing :

" *Mamma, mamma, lasciami andare la nella chiesa del buon*
      Signore,
   Colla   bocca   farò   preghiera   mentre   cogl'   occhi   farò
      l' amore ! "
   (Mama, mama, let me go to the church of the good
      Lord,
   While I am praying with the mouth I can make love
      with the eyes.)

CAROLINA'S STREET

II

CAROLINA sat at her loom weaving a web of flannel for the Sindaco's wife. The shuttle flew from one slim brown hand to the other with a rhythmical click-clack, click-clack that annoyed Giulio in his armchair by the fire.

"Art not nearly done ? " he growled. " Thou drivest me crazy with that noise."

" Have patience, my treasure ; the work is almost finished," said Carolina.

" Why slave thyself to death for that family ? I don't half believe Francesco means to marry thee. *Miserabile !* Wait till I get well, then let me catch him making eyes at thee ! "

" Do not excite thyself, beloved, or thou wilt bring on a coughing spell."

" What has the Sindaco, or his wife, or their son ever done for thee that thou shouldst care so much more for them than for thine own family, eh ? Answer me that, now."

Carolina's yarn snapped, the rhythmic move-
183

ment of the loom ceased. "Sometimes, brother mine, thou seemst more anxious for the marriage than I am myself," she said slowly.

"What! thou dost not wish to marry Francesco, after all the trouble I have been at to get the precious fellow for thee? Well, of all the ingrates!"

Carolina rose from her loom — there was no other way. Giulio was working himself into a frenzy of rage, — his usual method of getting his own way.

"Thou art right. I have done enough for to-day," she said gently. "Shall I heat a cup of milk, or beat up one of these nice fresh eggs for thee?"

"Women think of nothing but eating! Whatever ails a man they imagine they can satisfy him by feeding him. I hate the sight of food, dost hear? When I am hungry I will tell thee so."

Carolina drew a low stool to his side, and sat down to mend his heavy homespun coat. She had helped her grandfather raise and shear the sheep; she had carded and spun the wool and woven the cloth for it. The humpbacked tailoress, her aunt, who lived at Pescocostanzo, had cut out the coat. Carolina herself had made it up.

"Dost thou wish to aggravate me by the sight of that coat? Thou thyself saidst that the air had a touch of winter — once let that begin, and good-bye to my stirring out till I am well, or the cold weather over."

"The doctor says if thou wilt go out every day, no matter what the weather is, thou wilt not feel the cold. He even desires thee to sleep in the open air," said Carolina.

"Hangman of a doctor! If that did not kill me in a week, 't would be a miracle worthy of thy Madonna of Pietro Anzieri. "

"Hush, oh, hush!" whispered Carolina, as she crossed herself. "Where is thy young lieutenant? He who had the cough?"

"Gone back to Switzerland. His life is worth saving — he is a fine young imbecile, but he is a gentleman. My life! Who cares whether I live or die? The sooner I am under the sod the better for a girl whose *dote* is not large enough to satisfy that miserly cabbage-head Francesco."

" Switzerland — yes, that was the name." She repeated the word over and over.

"If those children — may they die of an apoplexy! — would only be quiet, I might get a nap now. Thou and the grandfather made such a noise last night I did not close an eye. It is perfectly heartless to snore so when thou know'st it keeps me awake."

Carolina made his ungracious head comfortable with a pillow, covered him with a blanket, and went out into the street. On the steps of the opposite house sat the midwife, a newly swaddled infant on her knees. Her three-year-old daughter stood beside her hugging a doll in swaddling clothes. Tina, Carolina's little cousin, came toddling over the round slippery cobblestones to meet her. Carolina fitted a pad upon her head and balanced her bronze concha upon it.

" Who goes with me to draw water at the fountain ? " she cried.

THE SINDACO'S HOUSE

HERMIT OF PIETRO ANZIERI

There was a chorus of " I, and I, and I," and of "Wait for me, Carolina!" as the children left their play and flocked about Carolina. In two minutes the street was empty, save for the midwife dozing on the steps; she could be trusted not to make a noise as long as the baby slept on her knee.

Roccaraso has two social centres, — the fountain where the women congregate, and the church steps where the men foregather. Carolina placed her concha on the worn pink granite curb of the fountain, sat down on the stone bench below, and unpinned her knitting from her rich braids of hair hidden by the fazzoletto. The children hovered about her like butterflies over a flower-bed.

The Sindaco's house — the best in the village — stands opposite the fountain. A small door opens into the underground cellar where the sheep live in winter; a handsome stone stairway leads to the front door high above the street. The carving of the marble balustrade, the shape of the windows, the elegance of the remaining bits of cornice, prove that it was

187

built before the rape of the Pescocostanzans (they carried off a daughter of the house), since when the family bleaches its linen at home — witness the sheet of creamy home-spun linen spread over the marble balustrade.

The Sindaco's wife, seeing Carolina from the window, joined her at the fountain.

" You are early, my dear," she said ; " how have you got on with my flannel to-day ? "

" Not so well as usual ; my loom is out of order. Better luck to-morrow ; you shall not be kept waiting for it, Matrina " (godmother).

" I saw the doctor coming out of your house yesterday. What did he say about Giulio ? "

The anxious look the children had driven away from Carolina's face came back like a cloud before the sun.

" He says that while there is life there is hope."

" Then your brother will not live through the winter. They told *me* that one month before my daughter died."

" Santa Maria ! You believe it ? "

" I have long feared it. Resign yourself, my child, to the will of God."

188

"Switzerland!" said Carolina; she had been trying to remember that hard word. Her needles clicked "Switzerland!" the fountain rippled "Switzerland!" every beat of her true heart throbbed "Switzerland!"

"Francesco should be back from the fair at Castel di Sangro soon; if he passes this way say that I wish to see him before he goes after the sheep."

"Surely, Matrina," Carolina replied.

A few minutes later when Francesco came up she did not see him; her eyes were fixed on the stocking she was knitting for Giulio; her thoughts were far away. Francesco stood looking at her, waiting till she should be aware of his presence.

Roffredo Ferrari, American citizen, sitting on the church steps watching through half-closed eyelids, saw all this.

"I promised to be a little mother to him," said Carolina, unconscious of both men's eyes, unconscious that she had spoken aloud.

"To whom did you make that promise?"

Carolina looked up with a start. "Is that

189

you, Francesco ? Matrina wishes to speak with you. I was only saying that when my mother died I promised her to be a little mother to Giulio."

" So you have been. Does he deny it ? Was it your fault his regiment was ordered to Africa — that he got sick there ? "

" It is as the blacksmith says," murmured Roffredo, apparently asleep in the sunshine on the church steps. " Carolina does not look at that peacock Francesco with the eyes of love. As for him, he is a stone ; he thinks only of her money ; may he die of an accident ! "

On the morning when Roffredo first saw Carolina coming out of the hermitage chapel Love descended upon him like a whirlwind, and she,— the beloved, for whose sake only life was desirable,— she never even looked at him. He hung about Roccaraso half the day, made friends with the blacksmith, to whom he promised to sell (on his departure for New York) the old flea-bitten gray horse inherited from his uncle, and the squash-colored phaeton — the pride of Pescocostanzo, the envy of Roc-

caraso — that carried the mails from Pescocostanzo to Rivisondoli. At night Roffredo sat
opposite Sor' Giacomo's cottage watching the
window of the room where instinct told him
Carolina lay.

After listening to Francesco for a few minutes,
Carolina rose, filled the concha, swung it with a
grand free movement to her head, and strode
down the steep street, a lovely living caryatid.

" *Felice notte,*" she said kindly to Francesco.

" *Felicissima notte,* Carolina ! "

Roffredo had gained during his thirteen years
in New York something more than American
citizenship, — he had gained a little of the American spirit. Since his return to Pescocostanzo
this spirit had made itself felt in a fine dis-
regard of traditions, a confidence in his ability
to settle his own affairs without the advice of
the Pescocostanzo graybeards. Until he had
seen Carolina he had carried things with a high
hand ; now everything was changed.

" Too proud even to look at me," he groaned.

" *Pazienza !* the time will come when I will
make her see me ! "

III

THE festa of the Madonna of Pietro Anzieri
was celebrated with great pomp. The hermitage chapel was hung with crimson brocade
draperies, decorated with flowers and green
boughs ; there were many candles on the altar
and in the fine crystal chandelier — brought all
the way from Isernia for the festa. A new
silver crown was tacked to the canvas of the
miraculous picture, over the Madonna's head.
The priest from Roccaraso celebrated high
mass at half-past ten, the Romito serving. He
wore a clean white linen cotta, trimmed with
handsome lace ; the altar cloth was bordered
with lace of the same pattern. The Sindaco's
wife recognized Carolina's handiwork. She was
not a devout woman. The sight of the lace and
linen from the big marriage chest that held
Carolina's *corredo* made her angry ; she re-
garded these things as belonging already to
Francesco.

13   193

Outside the chapel Roffredo, with waxed moustachios, a suit of Bowery clothes, and a red rose behind his ear, looked with an indulgent eye on the preparations for the festa. Red and white curtains hung before the door and across the façade. Little bundles of twisted brown paper filled with gunpowder and tied together by white string were laid six inches apart all the way down the hill leading to the hermitage. At twelve o'clock a procession headed by the priest marched out into the sunlight. The Romito walked next, carrying a blue satin banner embroidered with a representation of the picture. He was preceded by a group of little girls scattering flowers. Then came the miraculous picture borne on the shoulders of six stalwart peasants. The choir of men and boys followed. The women and girls brought up the rear. As the Madonna appeared at the door the train was fired, and the little paper bundles banged, banged in her honor. Roffredo had applied too late for the position of bearer; the places had been long engaged, the privilege paid for. When they reached the stone pine, half-way between the hermitage and the church of Roccaraso, the blacksmith, who was the last of the bearers, made a sign to Roffredo. Roffredo, straightening his broad shoulders, throwing out his chest, strutting like a peacock, slipped into the blacksmith's place. Though he did not look behind, he was sure Carolina saw him, and the step with which he trod the dusty road had a suggestion of the American cake walk.

Carolina, at the very end of the queue, a child tugging at each hand, was dressed in her best homespun skirt and blue bodice. She wore her mother's gold earrings and coral beads.

When the procession had marched around the village square, escorted the Madonna to make her annual visit to the church of Roccaraso, returned to the hermitage and restored the miraculous picture to its place, the congregation melted away. The Sindaco's wife waited outside the hermitage for Carolina, who remained kneeling before the altar after the rest had gone.

Carolina was very tired. Giulio had had a bad night, and she had hardly slept. Before him she had only brave smiles; here in the chapel she was free to weep her heart out. The memory of her mother mingled itself and became confused with her thought of Mary of the seven sorrows. She could not have told whether she spoke to her own mother or to the mother of Christ.

"If it be your wish that the money be drawn from the bank, that the land be sold, that my brother should go to Switzerland—let there be a sign!"

She raised her misty eyes to the miraculous picture; the resemblance to her mother had never before been so strong. The midday sun brought out the tarnished gold halo from the dark background and lighted the Madonna's face. To Carolina's longing eyes the miraculous picture smiled.

Her prayer was answered.

IV

WHEN Carolina came to the chapel door, her face wore an expression the Sindaco's wife had never before seen.

"*Buona festa, Matrina*," she said gently.

Something had happened to Carolina; she had a look of high resolve the godmother could not understand. The lecture upon the extravagance of wasting lace and fine linen on the Romito was postponed. Francesco might dream of a more ambitious marriage, a bride with a larger *dote*, — his mother meant to have Carolina for her daughter-in-law.

"If the girl has a fault," she told the Sindaco, "she is a little too handsome; for all that she is less vain than many a plain girl."

Roffredo Ferrari, loitering in the hermitage graveyard, knew — he could not have explained how — the exact moment when the heavy leather curtain was lifted and Carolina appeared on the threshold. He swayed to-

197

wards her as a tall tree is bent by a strong wind. His eyes hungry for the sight devoured her face like a flame; he felt himself grow cold.

"So might the blessed Virgin herself have looked!" he murmured.

Carolina's eyes met his eyes, and for the first time she understood what they said. She missed a step and stumbled; Roffredo sprang forward, caught her arm, and for one rapturous moment steadied her while she regained her balance. The silvery light in her face slowly changed to deep red, as if the full moon had turned into the sun.

"A thousand thanks, sir," she said gently.

He hesitated for a word. Before he found it she was far down the road walking with the Sindaco's wife.

"She has seen — at last! She has spoken!" He raised his arm above his head with a gesture of exultation.

"Hein? What did you say?" said the Romito, sourly.

"That I wish to make a small offering, *frate!*" Roffredo dropped a piece of money

198

into the battered Japanned tin box hanging by a strap from the Romito's birdlike neck; the old man caught the flash of the silver coin as it disappeared. It was long since any but copper coin had rattled in his box, — and, *mirabile dictu*, the silver piece was offered by a Pescocostanzan !

V

THE government doctor lived at Castel di Sangro. He would have preferred to live at Roccaraso, where the view is better, the air finer, the water purer. His wife — she was a Roman — said that people meant more to her than trees or mountains; that one air was as good as another; that she never drank water; if he must bury her alive, let it be in a decent market town like Castel di Sangro, not an inaccessible mountain fastness like Roccaraso.

The sun had set when the doctor tied his horse at the gate of Roccaraso. He had been riding all day from village to village and had come home late, to find a summons from Carolina.

" Why do you go ? You can do nothing for that poor fellow Giulio, and you are so tired," his wife said when she gave him the message.

" Perhaps I may do something," said the doctor.

The best remedy he brought to the three-roomed whitewashed cottage, with its floor of trodden earth, was the cordial of human kindness. He sat and talked to Carolina and Giulio till the wine of his strength was all out of the bottle.

He came out into the moonlight to find the familiar figure of a man hiding in the shadow of the opposite house. The doctor was very tired; he had stood that day at the doors of life and of death, and watched the passing of a soul through each; he was in no mood to make allowances for love's madness. He walked quickly, turned into the next street, faced hastily about and waited for his man, who, coming hastily around the corner, ran plump into his arms.

"Stand back! Who are you, and why do you follow me?" the doctor fiercely demanded.

"The streets are free to all, I believe," was the haughty answer.

"Not to an armed man who skulks behind a physician when he visits the sick. My Signora has heard of your conduct, my fine fellow;

to-morrow she will complain of you to the Sindaco."

"Your Signora ! The Signor Dottore is married, then ? It is truly to see the sick man he goes so often to Sor' Giacomo's house ? "

" For what other reason should I go ? "

" I thought it might be to see Carolina."

" And if it were, what is Carolina to you ? "

" Ah, saints and apostles, hear him ! She is heaven, she is hell ; she is all that there is in this world or the next."

The doctor softened. "So you are in love with Carolina? Did you come from America to look for a wife ? "

" Sir, to be frank with you, the thought never occurred to me. My uncle having died and made me his heir, I came back to Italy to claim my inheritance."

" You will remain in Pescocostanzo ? "

Roffredo threw back his great head and laughed. "*I* remain in Pescocostanzo ? No, no. This country is too slow for me. If it were not for that girl I should be in New York this minute. I am in the fruit business there, sir.

Yes, I have done very well; my partner will doubtless steal all my money and run away if I do not return soon. I do not care. All places are alike to me now. *Here* I sometimes catch a glimpse of Carolina, though I cannot get a word with her. The Sindaco's wife watches her as a cat watches a mouse. All the same I believe Carolina is not quite indifferent to me." He twirled his moustache, straightened his shoulders, and seemed in the moonlight to grow an inch taller. " If you, sir, would use your influence ? That animal Francesco is not worthy to tie her shoe ; besides— he is not *simpatico* to her."

" Carolina is going away from Roccaraso very soon," said the doctor.

" Maria ! Does she go out to service or to a convent ? "

" Neither ; she is going on a long journey with her brother. Later, my wife will find her a situation in Rome."

" It is true, then, what the blacksmith says. Carolina thinks that by selling her property and taking Giulio to Switzerland, she can save her brother's life? Is it right to let her do this thing when the man has death in his face?"

"The Sindaco's wife says it is not right. The Romito wishes Carolina to lay out the money in restoring the hermitage chapel. He says a miracle might be worked and Giulio's health restored; in any case, even if nothing came of it, the money would be spent among our own people."

"You, a physician, allow that angel to sacrifice her little fortune for that poor, diseased Giulio? What use is he to the world?"

"Carolina has as much right to buy a few more months of life for Giulio as if she were a queen."

"Money comes and goes easily with you gentlefolks. We peasants—" Roffredo began.

"Do you wish to marry Carolina?" the doctor interrupted impatiently.

"That is the most ardent desire of my soul."

"Can you support a wife?"

"I can do my share."

"Would you still wish to marry Carolina if she had not a penny?"

205

" Carolina is not poor."

" Listen ! If you want a wife with property, come no more to Roccaraso."

" I cannot understand," said Roffredo.

" Ah, well ! You do not know the Sindaco's wife. That old cat wants her Francesco to marry Carolina. She has great influence with the girl and with the grandfather, Sor' Giacomo. Carolina owns three fields, the cottage in which she lives, and four thousand francs invested in the *rendita*" (Government bonds). " While Carolina owns that property do you suppose the Sindaco's wife will allow her to marry any man except Francesco? But let Carolina spend all her money in trying to prolong Giulio's life, Francesco will refuse to marry her. Your only chance of getting the girl is to let the *dote* go."

" I understand you," said Roffredo, " but, *Corpo di Baccho!* it is a high price to pay."

" Nothing that is worth having is cheap." said the doctor. " *Buona notte*, go home and think it over. If you find the price too high take the next steamer for North America."

HERMIT OF PIETRO ANZIERI

" *Grazie, e scusi, Signor Dottore, e buon riposo,*" said Roffredo.

They parted at the crumbling gateway of Roccaraso, — the doctor to ride along the white highroad to Castel di Sangro ; Roffredo to walk through the valley where the golden gorse grows, and over the heathery hillside that leads to Pescocostanzo.

VI

IT was a blue and gold September day; the air was intoxicating with the rich savors of the harvest. Carolina was at work in her little triangular patch of ground on the sloping hillside above the Rasino. Here, in the spring, she had planted corn, wheat, potatoes, peas, and beans; through the hot summer she had faithfully weeded the soil and kept the vegetables free from insects. She had dug the potatoes, threshed the chaff from the grain, dried and shelled the peas and beans, and put all safely away in the upper chamber of the cottage, against the coming of the long winter. She had chosen this fine day, when the air had a dash of the elixir of the first cold, to plough the field for the winter wheat.

She usually sang at her work, to-day she was silent; there were hard lines about her mouth, a scowl on her forehead. This land, which for centuries her forbears had tilled, was to be sold ; the sacrifice had never seemed so great before. Dead hands reached out from the grave and clutched at the land — hers by the bitter toil, the grinding economies of generations of peasants.

What she sowed another would reap ; the thought struck cold upon her. If she could be sure of seeing Giulio strong and well again, nothing would matter, but if he should die and the sacrifice be all in vain?

So the devil — or her forefathers — tempted her.

" *Mammina, mammina !* " (little mamma). She threw a supplicatory hand above her head.

" Ah ! *bestia infame !* " (infamous beast). She knocked her forehead with her closed fist, spat upon the ground, and grasped the handles of the plough.

" Courage, my girl, courage ! " she cried.

Ploughing had never seemed such hard work before ; when she had finished a third of the triangle she stopped, rested her arms on the plough, and stood looking down into the new-turned furrow of moist brown earth. She did not hear Roffredo's footsteps as he came towards her; they were deadened by the soft loam. The handles of the plough were taken from her hands, and a strange voice said, —

"Give me the plough; this is no woman's work."

"No, no, sir! What an idea! I only stopped a moment to take breath."

Roffredo threw all his weight against the handles. The soil was stubborn; the plough needed sharpening. At first he drove it clumsily enough. Carolina followed him step by step, remonstrating.

That was a spur; the work began to go better.

"There, that will do. What you have done will be a great help. One sees that you have not the habit of working in the fields. You will feel the sun on your head," Carolina besought.

"Peace! When the work is done we will talk," Roffredo answered firmly.

Carolina's eyes opened wide at the tone of authority.

TWO IN ITALY

The last furrow ploughed, Roffredo tossed back his brown curls, wiped the sweat from his forehead, and joined Carolina sitting on a large stone at the edge of the field.

" Now let us talk," he said.

" Willingly." As she made no room for him on the stone, he threw himself on the ground beside her.

" Look at me," he begged of her. With a blush like the dawn she turned her eyes (they were like cool, brown agates) to his.

" Carolina, you are as beautiful as the Madonna; perhaps you are as good, who knows? You have no parents. Sor' Giacomo, your grandfather, is childish; your brother is ill; your godmother wishes to poison me. In the country where I come from," he pointed with a large gesture to the west, " the young people settle these things for themselves; it is perhaps the better way. Carolina, will you have me for your husband ? "

" *Ma che*," said Carolina, " do not jest about serious things."

" Listen, my angel, and do not interrupt.

212

Nothing could be more serious. When the doctor comes this afternoon ask him freely of me. I have opened my heart to him; he knows my circumstances; he will tell you if you may with discretion accept me."

"Roffredo, you are a stranger."

"You know my name?"

"My aunt the tailoress — she with the hump — lives at Pescocostanzo. I know something of you," she began to explain.

"One thing you cannot know, *amore ma bella* — because the words are not yet invented strong enough to tell — how I love you! *Pazienza*, I will show you some day."

"Love! It is so easy to talk of love to a girl. We have not spoken till to-day : it would be a miracle."

"Don't you know love is the greatest miracle? The first time I saw you, you had been praying the Madonna for a miracle. Well, she has shown you the greatest of all!"

"Roffredo, as you have guessed, I am not quite indifferent to you. If I were free — but

I am not. I have vowed to devote my life to my poor sick brother."

"Carolina, hear me. I will respect that vow. I will help to care for your brother."

"No, no, it is not possible."

"To-morrow the furrow will be ready for the seed ; when you come to plant I shall be here."

"No, no!" Still she lingered. In the end it was Roffredo who bade her go.

"Depart now," he said, "or that old cat, your godmother, will wonder what has kept you so long."

"*Ahimé!* I am a wicked wretch. It is late for Giulio's soup," Carolina cried.

She ran lightly down the hill, through the meadow where the linen lay bleaching in the sun, disappeared in the thicket, coming out on the other side with a huge load of fagots on her head.

Now she moved slowly, with the cautious step of the burden bearer. Warily, painfully she tested every step, planting her feet solidly among the rolling stones of the steep path that leads from the valley to the town gate.

HERMIT OF PIETRO ANZIERÍ

In his childhood Roffredo had often seen his old grandmother, his mother, his little sisters carrying fagots and thought nothing of it. His point of view had changed; a deep satisfying oath rumbled from the neighborhood of his boots:

"Dogs and sons of dogs, to use your women so! The men of Pescocostanz' did well to carry off the girls from such as you — may you all die squashed!"

VII

THE cold fell early that year; before September was gone the nights grew chill and Giulio grew worse. Preparations for departure began in earnest. Roffredo, now openly Carolina's suitor, found her one morning on her knees before an old hair-covered trunk studded with brass-headed nails. An immense green carpet-bag, flowered with red roses, was already packed with her belongings.

"You are really going?" cried Roffredo.

"She will have it so," said poor Giulio, his eyes bright with the hope of life. "Nothing satisfies this foolish one but to take me to Davos-Platz."

"You have a good sister."

"She knows there is really nothing serious the matter with me. That good Swiss air will soon set me up. This is a vile climate, as you yourself know."

"I have heard you say that it did not

217

suit you," Roffredo murmured. Carolina had warned him that Giulio must never be contradicted; a difference of opinion always brought on a coughing spell. " It is a long journey."

"The longer it is the further it will take me from this hole," said Giulio. Roffredo, watching Carolina, saw her blanch at the words " a long journey."

There was a knock at the door, and the Sindaco's wife bounced into the room, red with anger at the news the midwife had brought her that Carolina was actually packing up to go.

"You are really going? Alas! if your poor mother were only alive! It is madness; it is ruin! I never heard of such a thing as a young woman going travelling alone with a young man. What will people think? It is not respectable ! "

" My grandfather is willing; Giulio desires to go; it is only you, dear Matrina, who object. I am sorry to distress you, but I know from the blessed Virgin herself that my mother in Paradise who sees and hears me wishes

me to go to Switzerland with my poor
Giulio."

"Sor' Giacomo is no better than a child; as
to that government doctor, I have my opinion
of him. What does he mean by coming pok-
ing his nose into our affairs, taking the part of
an unreasonable boy and a foolish girl!"

Giulio (his chief pleasure in life was to bait
the Sindaco's wife) said to her innocently,
"*You* ought to feel for me! You remember
that I was once as strong as Roffredo here
— see what muscles he has, a perfect ox of a
man — I believe I could have thrashed him in
those days. But your Francesco was always
puny and rickety. I remember my mother
(of blessed memory) making me promise not
to let the other boys hurt him. Ah! I have
fought many a battle on his account."

At that moment Francesco coming in shook
his fist in the sick man's face.

"So you are taking Carolina away, just as
we were going to arrange things comfortably
between us? Suppose anything should happen
to you, what would become of her?"

Carolina was for once off guard. She had stepped into the street and was talking with Roffredo.

"After all she has done for you a pretty gratitude you show!" scolded the Sindaco's wife.

"Do you suppose I would go if I were not perfectly sure I should recover my health in Switzerland?" growled Giulio. "Until Carolina has a husband it is my duty to take care of her; to do this I must first get well."

"How will she get a husband if you take her away to this strange place?"

"When a bridegroom comes to claim her I will talk with him," said Giulio, sourly.

"If you reduce your sister to beggary, where can she hope to find a bridegroom?" cried the woman in a great passion.

"Ha, ha!" laughed Giulio; "so that's the matter? You grudge me my life! You wish to hurry me to my grave that you may enjoy my inheritance! Truly, a nice family to marry into. Dost thou hear, Carolina? Francesco and his mother desire us to remain

in Roccaraso, so that when the "white" comes
and the earth freezes thou mayst put me
under it and he may make merry spending
my money."

Carolina ran to his side, stroked his hand,
wiped the sweat from his forehead.

"Do not agitate thyself, *amor mio*. Matrina, I think you had better go," she said.
"He does not know what he says when he is
angry. Do not remember it against him."

Without another word the Sindaco's wife
and son flung angrily out of the cottage.

"Good riddance to bad rubbish!" Giulio
called after them. "Carolina, at what time
didst thou say our train started?"

"At noon to-morrow, my treasure. Drink
this good milk and cognac now and eat a good
supper, so as to sleep well and be strong for
the journey."

Roffredo, watching the sister and brother
from the doorway, groaned at the thought of
what that journey might hold. An immense
pity and tenderness filled his heart. A thousand wild schemes surged through his brain by

which the journey might be prevented. Yet he knew that Carolina was immovable; that she had pledged herself to lead that forlorn hope to victory or to death, and that she would keep her vow, cost what it might.

Carolina was on foot early the next morning. When she first looked out of the cottage door a thick white mist filled the valley of the Rasino, completely hiding Il Gran Sasso, the tall blue mountain which serves the village of Roccaraso as a barometer. As the sun sucked up the earth's vapors, the mist veil lifted and showed the top of the mountain all ruddy with a deep glow reflected from the rising sun.

"There is no cloud cap on the Gran Sasso this morning," said Carolina, consulting the mountain barometer; "we shall have a fine, bright day, *grazie Deo!*"

While Carolina brought water from the fountain and fagots from the woodpile, filled the kettle and lighted the fire, the mountain's veil of mist dropped lower and lower — as the veil of a bride is dropped — till all its glorious outline, peak and sides and foot, stood revealed, a shining splendor in the morning world.

There was still time before Giulio would wake to keep her tryst with Roffredo at the hermitage, make a parting prayer to the Madonna, and take leave of the Romito.

She found Roffredo waiting for her in the hermitage graveyard; he was standing before an ancient blue slate tombstone with a cherubim's head and an hour-glass carved above the name and the date, 1404. Coming up softly from behind, Carolina touched him on the arm, surprising him as he had surprised her at her ploughing, in the early days of their love, nearly a month ago.

"Blood of my heart, is it thou? I thought the morning was too bright for mere sunlight." Roffredo whispered the words, though no one but their two selves was within earshot.

"*Amor mio!* Tell me what is written on the stone. I know that this is the name, but what do those other words mean?" She touched the worn letters with a hand that trembled.

TWO IN ITALY

Roffredo clasped her strong brown hand, the honest hand that had worked so faithfully at the loom and at the plough, as he read aloud the epitaph:

> *" Guardi passaggier del tuo fin la sorte,*
> *Qual tu sei io fui, ed or in polve*
> *Torna il tuo corpo frale, e si risolve,*
> *E qual son' io, tu pur sarai in morte ! "*

Carolina shivered at the words, as common in Italy as the equivalent —

> " Stranger, pause as you pass by.
> As you are now, so once was I ;
> As I am now, so you will be.
> Prepare for death and follow me ! "

in New England.

She drew her shawl about her, and for comfort pressed closer to her lover's side.

" Roffredo, I do not want to die," she murmured.

" Thou art not going to die ; at least not for a long time ! " he exclaimed, with a fine air of protection.

" But I don't *ever* want to die ! "

"Ah, well, when thou art a hundred years old thou mayst feel differently. Go in now, core of my heart, and say thy prayers. I will wait here for thee. There comes thine uncle, the Romito, to keep me company."

Roffredo spoke cheerily. Carolina looked up into his face and smiled wanly. On the chapel steps she ran into the Romito, who was coming down.

Though it was no festa and not yet seven o'clock, the hermit was clean shaven; his rusty black gown showed large wet spots where he had tried to clean it; his shoes were blacked; he had an air of reckless gayety that struck Carolina.

"Hast thou forgotten that we part to-day?" She spoke to the Romito, she looked at Roffredo. The Romito rolled his large sheepish eyes at her.

"Ah! my dear, we must keep up thy spirits," he said.

"Remember, Romito," Roffredo whispered fiercely, as the leathern curtain fell behind Carolina, "you are to go to Pescocostanzo with us!"

TWO IN ITALY

"I never said I would go!" the old fellow answered firmly.

"With respect, you are as obstinate as an ass! It is the only way," Roffredo persisted.

"How can you ask me to drive with you to Pescocostanzo, my son?" whined the hermit. "The Pescocostanzans are persons without faith and of little education. Their conduct towards Our Lady of Pietro Anzieri, whose poor servant I am, has always been barbarous, not to say sacrilegious. It is thirty years since I have set foot in that town; you may not know this."

"It is not your fault if I do not know it; you have told me often enough. Without compliments, you *must* come. You have great influence with Carolina; she will listen to you. Romito, were you ever in love?"

The hermit looked carefully about him to see that they were alone; then, standing on tiptoe and stretching his long yellow neck, he whispered in Roffredo's ear. The young man clapped him gayly on the shoulder, crying, —

"Eh? Truly? Bravo! *galantuomo! You*

can understand that it is impossible for me
to separate from Carolina. She cannot write
me; she cannot read my letters. In the
name of all the saints, why was that girl not
taught to read or write?"

"When the government school was opened
in Roccaraso, the father being dead, the mother
asked my advice about sending her children to
school. I remember that I said to her, 'Send
the boy if you will, but do not send the girl.
If your daughter learns to write she will de-
ceive you when she grows up; she will be
forever writing to young men.'"

Roffredo groaned. "If she *could* only write
to *this* young man!"

The Romito looked offended. "Carolina has
been taught all that it is necessary for a woman
to know of books," he said. "She can repeat
the rosary, the litany, and the catechism; she
can make all the responses in the mass; what
does she want with reading and writing?"

"My little sister, Piccina," said Roffredo,
"not ten years old, has learned to read, to
write, and many other things; she can read

music by note, and she draws quite nicely already."

"And where has she learned all these fine things?" asked the Romito, scornfully.

"In an American school, which they call the garden of the children."

"What nonsense!" cried the Romito. "I maintain that a neater, sweeter, better educated girl than my niece Carolina does not exist; if this were not so, would you be so anxious to marry her?"

"Hush! there she comes, looking more like a Madonna than ever," whispered Roffredo.

Carolina's eyes had that expression of exaltation they always wore after a visit to the Madonna of Pietro Anzieri. She came down the steps calm and strong.

"Farewell, *carissimo*," she said; "let us part here, where we first met, outside the chapel of the Madonna."

"Heart of my heart, thou and I must never part again. At Pescocostanzo the priest is waiting to marry us; the magistrate, my cousin, to make the civil marriage. The Romito here has given his consent. He wishes to go with us in order to represent thy family at these ceremonies."

"Liar, prevaricator, perjurer, I have refused!" the hermit shouted, then paused; neither of the lovers was listening to him.

"Roffredo, I swear to be true to thee. I will marry no other," Carolina was saying, "not Francesco, no, if he should come to ask me on his knees, with his hands full of diamonds and pearls. I would die for thee, but I will not abandon my poor brother for thee."

"I swear to thee that as long as Giulio lives, not only thou but I myself will care for him."

"No, no, the sacrifice is too great, I cannot allow it."

"*Taci!*" (be silent). Holding fast to her hand Roffredo led Carolina, followed by the Romito, to the back of the hermitage, where stood an ancient flea-bitten gray horse and a prehistoric squash-colored phaeton.

"Behold the equipage! Behold the mail! The contract my uncle made to carry the mails, which since his death I have held, expires to-day. If the mail-bags are not delivered without further delay, I shall forfeit the last payment still due me — I may even be fined, possibly put in prison."

Poor Carolina gasped at the word " prison." " Uncle," she cried desperately, " what shall I do ? "

" Carolina *mia*, since you have sacrificed your patrimony to make this mad journey, I tell you frankly you can no longer pick and choose a bridegroom, as was formerly the case when you had a better dowry than any girl in Roccaraso. It seems that Roffredo has brought back strange ideas from North America, where the marriage customs appear to be quite barbarous, parents feeling it no shame to send a daughter without even a *soldo* — yes, quite as a beggar — to her husband's house. It is lucky for us all that Roffredo is willing to marry you on these terms, but such haste as he proposes is shocking, not to say indecent."

" *Andiamo !* " cried Roffredo. " Carolina, sit here beside me. Romito, get in behind there. Squat upon the smaller mail-bag, embrace the other so "thou wilt not fall out." The Romito, a leaf in the storm, was whirled into the chariot, his long thin shanks doubled under him, his thin arms clasping convulsively a large leather sack of newspapers.

"*Madonna mia!* The man is mad!" he whimpered.

The gray stamped its hind foot to kick off a fly. The Romito shrieked, "San Antonio, protect us! Get in, Carolina. Roffredo is possessed! After the manner of the Pescocostanzans he carries you off by force, without ceremony!"

"Thou meanest what thou hast said?" asked Carolina. She sounded her lover's eyes and found them honest.

"Thou art a good man." She climbed into the phaeton. Roffredo sprang after her, snapped his aged whalebone whip; the gray horse started with a jump, and the old yellow phaeton, the pride of Pescocostanzo, the envy of Roccaraso, lurched down the white highroad in the direction of Pescocostanzo.

VIII

Giulio, too much absorbed in the coming journey to think long of anything else, received Carolina and Roffredo as if what had happened was the most natural thing in the world.

"So you two are married? Truly, Carolina, thou art a little witch; nothing could have been more fortunate. Roffredo here is strong enough to carry all our baggage, and to lend me an arm into the bargain."

"Oh, yes, I am strong enough for the whole family," cried Roffredo, as he shouldered the green flowered carpet-bag. Carolina stooped down to pick up the hair-covered trunk, preparatory to placing it on her head.

"Wait a minute, Madama," cried Roffredo, "here is one who will bear that burden for thee." A strong young lass received the trunk upon her head and swung off with it to the station.

" That is a waste of money ; she will want five soldi for taking that trunk to the station," sighed Carolina.

" Ah, well, one may be extravagant on one's wedding day," laughed Roffredo. His good-nature was contagious. They all laughed together.

" Thou shalt never again carry such burdens on thy beautiful head, that I promise thee," he whispered.

Carolina looked at him with grave, wondering eyes and shook her beautiful head. She loved Roffredo with all the passion of a first love, but she did not pretend to understand him.

On the way to the station they were joined by the Romito and the government doctor. Giulio, leaning on his brother-in-law's arm, nodded gayly to them.

" A plague on this street," he cried ; " if it were not so steep we should have the pleasure of driving past the Sindaco's house in Roffredo's carriage. The carriage is waiting for us at the sheepfolds at the foot of the hill. That old cat is watching us from the housetop. She will see us drive up to the station, *grazie Deo.*"

They had no more time than was necessary to buy their tickets and weigh their baggage.

" I shall send all these things in the luggage van," Roffredo declared.

" What madness! There are but fourteen pieces, even counting the basket of provisions, the fiascone of wine, and the box of eggs," cried Carolina.

" There will be plenty of room in the racks for all these things; it will cost a fortune to send them as luggage," Giulio objected.

" Not for that old hair-covered trunk with the brass nails; where did it come from?" cried Roffredo.

" It is the best trunk; quite as good as the day it came into the house with grandmother's *corredo,*" said Carolina, firmly.

" It is so strange looking!" objected Roffredo.

" When one travels it is not necessary to *fare figura,*" said the Romito. " One is among strangers; nobody knows one."

TWO IN ITALY

The train coming in sight at this moment ended the argument. Roffredo had his way about the haircloth trunk ; the other thirteen pieces were crowded into the racks, which fortunately were quite empty.

The moment for parting came. Carolina, grown pale, swallowed back the tears as she took leave of her uncle and the government doctor.

" *Addio, dottore mio*, may the Madonna reward you ! " she said.

" Good-bye, everybody. I shall be back in time for the spring planting," Giulio called cheerfully from the window.

" *A rivederci, dottore*," said Roffredo, " when Giulio has no more need of us Carolina and I shall sail for New York. If you ever come there my store is in Mulberry Street; anybody can tell you where it is."

"*Grazie mille, e rivederci*," cried the doctor.

As the train started poor Giulio was seized with a terrible spasm of coughing.

" It 's a good thing that Carolina has that stout young fellow along to help her," said the doctor, waving his hat as the train steamed across the valley of the golden gorse, in the direction of Pescocostanzo. He and the Romito had been left together on the platform.

"Hein?" said the hermit. "What was that you once said to me about being too busy to make marriages? If Carolina has a husband it is thanks to you."

"Nonsense," said the doctor. "I had nothing to do with it." He dropped a piece of money into the Romito's begging box.

"For yourself, understand, to drink the bride's health."

"I shall not fail to do so; yours as well. I shall also buy candles for Our Lady, and burn them with a petition that she continue her protection of Carolina. Terrible as it is to cross the ocean to North America, it is better than having to live at Pescocostanzo, for Roffredo, after all, is now an American and not a Pescocostanzan."

* * * * * * *

In Mulberry Street, the heart of New York's "Little Italy," is a fine fruit and wine store kept by Roffredo Ferrari and his handsome wife Carolina. Next door is the "Tonsorial Parlor" of her brother Giulio (now called Julian). Thanks to the Madonna of Pietro Anzieri, to the good Swiss air, or to Carolina's indomitable will, the miracle was accomplished and Giulio's health restored. Carolina rules both establishments with the firm hand of a benevolent despot. She has a word to say about most things in the little Abruzzi colony within the larger Italian colony. She is Father Oberto's right hand ; the good priest recognizes that hers is the ruling spirit in the "block," honeycombed with dwellings of the Ferrari's friends and relations who have followed them across the ocean, through the Gate of Hope, to the Hospitable Land.

VIII

IN OLD POLAND

.

CHAPTER VIII

IN OLD POLAND

I

"I WAIT!" said the gorgeous being; his beauty took away my breath. He was young and tall; he wore a uniform of white broadcloth, a shining helmet and cuirass, high boots coming above the knee, and a big sabre swinging at his side. He was even handsomer than his dress, a blond giant with fair hair, pink cheeks, blue eyes, and an adorable little golden moustache.

"I wait!" he repeated haughtily.

There was not room to pass on the narrow strip of dry pavement; one of us must step out into the puddle on either side. His insolence restored the breath his beauty took away.

"I also wait!"

16   241

TWO IN ITALY

His angry scorn did not consume me ; remembering Ethan Allen and the olive, I stood
my ground. He eyed me for one intolerable
moment ; a trumpet sounded from the barrack
across the square — perhaps he was late for
parade or drill, for at the sharp tara-tara, with
one muttered word "*Americanischer !*" he
stepped out into the dirty water (it closed over
his wonderful boots, splashed his immaculate
breeches) and was gone, a splendid pink and
gold vision of wrath I shall not forget. I was
grieved at the spotting of that fine raiment.
Had he shown the least courtesy, appealed,
even with a look, to my good fellowship — but
no, he had arrogantly ordered me out of his
path as an inferior !

That was our first impression of Berlin, of
Prussian Junkerism. It was all in keeping
with the tradition of my father's reception here
in 1831. He had come to study the methods
of teaching at the School for the Blind. On
his way from Boston to Berlin he stopped in
Paris, where he fell in with General Lafayette.
We have the General's letter asking my father

to meet him on a certain day, the day that
business was arranged which caused my father
to be arrested in his hotel at Berlin on the
night of his arrival, under the *lettre de cachet*
system, and shut up in prison for five weeks
without trial or hearing. Lafayette had asked
him to make a *détour* on his way to Berlin to
a place on the banks of the Vistula, and to
carry a large sum of money, subscribed by
American citizens, to clothe and feed the
Polish refugees (chiefly women and children)
who were there suffering terrible hardships while
the last remnant of fighting men were making
their final heroic stand for national existence.
The dangerous commission safely executed, my
father pushed on to Berlin on his inoffensive
mission. I have heard him tell of the arrogance of the two *gens d'armes* who escorted
him on his long drive from Berlin to the
Belgian frontier, where, he used to say, they
kicked him out of the country with a warning never to return. *Now* I know just how
those traditionary *gens d'armes* looked and
behaved.

TWO IN ITALY

Berlin on the Emperor's birthday is a gay place. In the morning came the review of the troops. I saw my officer riding at the head of his men; he is a lieutenant of the *garde du cour.* Of all those splendid soldiers I think the White Uhlans the most imposing, though the Dragoons with their bearskins, the Hussars with their preposterous caps, and jackets dangling from their shoulders, are as handsome in their way.

The horses are worthy of the riders; well bred, sleek (a horse can sometimes afford to be sleek, a man never), with long flowing tails, crinkled manes, handsomely saddled and bridled, with particularly nice saddle cloths.

"Those chaps," said J. (the infantry were filing by), "are the backbone — the real stuff of the army. Every battle from Marathon to Sedan has been decided by the staying power of the rank and file."

"I hate," said Virginia, "the way they throw out their legs, more like ostriches marching than like men."

"You women folk are all the same,"

grumbled J.; "you never have eyes for any-thing but cavalry!"

Our hotel was near the barracks. Every morning we were waked by a melodious liquid sound as of a rushing torrent turning over the loose stones of a river bed. At the noise Virginia and I sprang up, ran to the window to watch the passing regiment; to see the torrent of horses pacing in perfect time, their beautiful heads bobbing back and forth, their feet stepping to the joyous measure of the bugle; to see, incidentally, the officers. Horses and men were like a company of shining centaurs; as fresh and well-liking as if the pinky glow in the sky over Unter den Linden shone from the setting, not the rising sun. The career of arms leads to one victory at least, — a victory of the will, — the habit of early rising.

The evening after the review we saw a gala performance at the opera-house of a famous ballet, the Puppen Fee; it costs so much to produce that it is only given on occasions like this, when the Emperor takes the whole theatre and invites the court, the military and diplomatic circles, to be his guests. The theatre was crowded with those magnificent officers and their ladies, all in the fullest of full dress, sparkling with jewels and orders. There was hardly a black coat in the house outside of the box of the American ambassador, where we sat. I saw the Kaiser distinctly. His face is keen, alert, full of vitality. I am sure he is perfectly sincere in his belief in the divine rights of kings, of the King of Prussia especially. His poor withered arm, root of so much sorrow, of such bitterness between his mother and himself, was held close to his side. They say the Emperor believes the injury was received at birth, blames the English physician, and never forgave the Empress Frederick for calling in the Britisher instead of employing a German doctor.

The first time I was in Germany the old Emperor William was on the throne, with his "faithful servant" Bismark at his right hand. The Emperor Frederick was the nation's adored "Unser Fritz," and the Empress Frederick *his* beloved Crown Princess. They were a fine couple; I remember them well; he was a blond, handsome, hearty man; she had the distinction that belonged to all Queen Victoria's daughters. I once saw the Crown Princess riding at the head of the Prussian regiment of which she was honorary Colonel. She wore the gay cap and jacket of the regimental uniform, and a plain black habit skirt; in spite of the petticoat she was a gallant figure. The Empress Frederick brought many civilizing influences with her from England to Prussia. I found a pretty illustration of this in the " Life of Rosa Bonheur." In 1870, when the German army was marching on Paris, their route, as originally laid down, led through the village where Rosa Bonheur, the famous French animal painter, lived. When it was known that the Germans were coming, the great little woman, in her male attire, insisted upon doing sentinel duty with the men of the village. When the hated German battalions came in sight, she was on guard, musket on shoulder, holding the bridge.

The battalions came; they passed. Avoiding the village, they marched by on the opposite bank of the Seine to a bridge lower down the river. Later it was learned that the commanding general had received a telegram from the Crown Princess, asking him to spare the home of Rosa Bonheur the ignominy of a visit from the conquerors. Isn't that a nice personal touch? In her girlhood she must have admired the pictures her mother bought from the painter. I think Queen Victoria owned among others that lovely picture of Scotch cattle in a Highland mist.

After the dear pretty soldiermen — yes, in spite of all, we admired them — the Museum is the best thing we found in Berlin. It is glorious, with a collection of Greek and Roman statues ranking next to that of the Vatican at Rome. Here I saw at last the original bronze statue of the Praying Boy, after having loved him all my life in photographs and casts. The statue was found at the bottom of the Tiber in Rome — my dear yellow river — and carried off to Berlin. You can imagine how

— in the midst of all that was alive and modern — it felt to come across this beautiful Greek statue in the cold and silent halls of the Museum.

In spite of the soldiers and the statues we were not sorry to leave Berlin. Just as we were asking each other " Where next ? " came an invitation from our old friend Gertrude — married and buried alive in that part of old Poland now called West Prussia — to visit her in her German home. It is a long expensive journey, as the burial place is near the borders of Russia, only half as far again from St. Petersburg as it is from Berlin. To get there we should pass over the ground my father covered when he carried aid to the Poles. We should see the Vistula.

" Be sure," said Gertrude's letter, " to come by the gilt-edged limited, *first class;* be sure to wear your best bib and tucker."

I consulted Bradshaw's Continental Railway Guide; what is more (class me with Herodotus), I understood it !

" The difference between first and second

class tickets would buy seats for the play of
" Faust," which we have never seen — probably
shall never have another chance to see. It's
absurd extravagance ! Only royalty, fools, and
Americans travel first class in Germany.

" Wear my new blue hopsack suit on an all-
night journey ? " said Virginia, " nenni ! "

We follow the old Englishwoman's rule of
three dresses for a traveller : Hightum for best,
Tightum for second best, Scrub for rainy days
and journeys.

" Gertrude knows we travel second in Germany (in France and Italy first is only just
good enough); she has a reason for what she
asks. Let's compromise : though Scrub is
good enough, wear Tightum, go by a slow
train second to X, wait there for the limited,
travel the rest of the way first."

We went to " Faust," wonderful as an acted
play, with the black poodle, the devil, the trans-
formation of Dr. Faustus the philosopher into
Faust the lover, all in the first act. We are so
used to Gounod's opera that we almost forget
it is a mere shadow of Goethe's masterpiece.

IN OLD POLAND

All fell out as we had planned as far as X. If the express had been on time, we should have made a close connection with just enough leeway to buy our deceitful first-class tickets and re-check our luggage. Alas! the gilt-edged was late. Followed a grim hour passed in the desolate first-class waiting-room, an enormous barn of a place with red plush thrones, a bust of the Kaiser, oil chromo portraits of his father and mother in their youth.

Nobody had waited in the cold splendor of the first-class waiting-room at X since the last royalty passed through six weeks before. The restaurant was closed, the ticket seller dozed, even the fierce military telegraph operator in his gold-laced uniform slept in his cage, his head bent over his machine, which clicked, clicked incessantly, only his own particular click having the power to wake him. It was that dreadful hour before dawn when the earth's chill gets into one's bones if one happens not to be in bed where one belongs.

Running up and down the platform to get warm, we caught the big yellow eye of the

Cyclops coming at us down the straight rails. A minute later at Cyclops' snort, the drowsy station sprang into discordant life, like the Sleeping Beauty's palace at the Prince's kiss. The station master thought he owed us a grudge because we had caught him engaged with a sandwich and a glass of schnapps. He did not know how hungry we were, how *un*filling at the price were the chocolates in tinfoil from the pfennig in the slot-machine — how we envied him his frankfurter and *petit pain.*

The guard was crosser than two sticks. " First-class passengers at X ? *Wunderlich!* " He had never heard of such a thing. He ran along the knifeboard of the train looking into carriage after carriage — no room for us anywhere.

" There must be a great many royalties, Americans, or fools on board this train," said Virginia, " I wonder which ? "

" It will leave X with at least two fools more," I said. " If only J. had not stayed in Berlin ! "

" Ah, he *has* a way with these railroad kings,"

said Virginia. "I wonder if he could have handled this one!"

All this time the cross guard was fuming, muttering "*Donner wetter*," hopping up and down, peering into window after window. Virginia and I followed humbly.

"You are already more than an hour late, what keeps you?" hectored the station master.

"*Sonderbar!* Whoever expects first-class passengers at **X**? Tumble in here, there are only two in this carriage." Cyclops puffed and panted to be off, the bell rang impatiently, the guard fitted a key, threw open a door, and pitched us and our belongings pell-mell into the dark interior of a private saloon carriage.

"Oh, take care of that basket!" I implored.

"The basket be —!" roared the guard, and slammed the door just as the train started with a jolt.

There was an angry growl. "What is the matter?" A long gray figure, stretched at full length on the seat, sat up from a nest of travelling rugs.

"I beg your pardon," I groaned. "The

253

guard threw the basket in. I told him to be careful."

"Selby, drop that cursed lamp-shade, put up the curtain; let us have a little light."

"Yes, my lord."

Now light was the last thing I wanted, for, shame of shames, that dreadful basket — a palmetto knapsack basket we bought in Santo Domingo — had turned upside down (it always does in critical moments) and discharged its outrageous contents over the sleeping form of an English Milord, travelling with his secretary in a private car. As soon as Milord realized that the intruders were women, he softened.

"Allow me to assist you."

He handed me a pair of Virginia's tiny satin shoes and the yellow lacquered tea-caddy, and gathered together the lumps of sugar — oh, shame! The lemons — oh, despair! the candle ends! The knapsack basket served as an omnium gatherum of "human warious." At the eleventh hour, when the hotel omnibus stood at the door, the tea equipage and everything that had been forgotten were hurriedly collected and thrust into it. I worked off some of my purgatory — years of it, it seemed to me. As to Virginia — she is of an age when such mortifications bite to the bone.

Milord was of no consequence, Virginia thought, because he was old and fat. His secretary was young, with deep blue near-sighted eyes and pretty curling brown hair all rumpled by the sleep from which we had rudely roused him. They politely gave us seats near the window out of which we looked steadily as the train tore along. The morning was cold and damp, a wet tangible mist walled us into our carriage; stare as we might, we saw nothing but mist, mist, with now and then a ghostlike puff of white smoke from the engine drifting past the darkened windows. At every mile-stone a lone figure loomed through the fog, — a railway sentry stiffly presenting arms with a furled signal flag. This to show that the next mile of track for which he is responsible is clear. A good system! But when you come to system you must stop criticising the

Prussians. The effects of the military training are seen everywhere, in the very woodpiles arranged with a mathematical nicety I have never seen. When I first remember Germany, this was not so. I don't *like* militarism rampant, but the devil must have his due; I must say it has spruced up the nation astonishingly.

The Englishmen's luggage was quite as queer as ours, when it was daylight and we could see it. They travelled with a clock, a silver reflector candlestick hooked into the back of the seat, several air pillows, two Japanese hells (warming-pans), an enormous demijohn of water, and a tin box of biscuits.

"The *herrschaft* are warned not to get off at the next station," said the guard. "Owing to our being late,"— he glared at us as if it were all our fault, — "the usual ten minutes' stop for breakfast at the buffet station will be omitted."

"I would give," said Milord, "half a sovereign for a cup of tea.'

"If you can take your tea with lemon, you shall have it for nothing — if that water is the kind that makes tea," I said.

"It's just ordinary decent spring water," said the secretary.

"You have tea?" Milord's eyes brightened with the question.

"Tea, sugar, matches, lemons, alcohol, and an etna, as you have seen."

"If you would be so awfully kind — we have biscuits."

Virginia opened her green silk bag. "Here are chocolates from the penny-in-the-slot machine at X; perhaps they are more wholesome stale."

The tragedy of the tea equipage in the palm-leaf basket was turned to victory. We intruders became life-savers. The Englishmen's hearts warmed towards us. The meal though variegated was comforting. I wish you could have seen Milord's struggle to drink his tea in the cup of his silver whiskey flask without hitting the tip of his long beak. It was a good deal better than a play because it was

real. Soon we were all talking merrily together, Milord and I about diving-suits (he
has invented a new one), Virginia and the secretary about Eight's Week at Oxford, when
the cross guard called out, —

"Potztausand is the next station."

We put our things hastily together.

"You get out *here?*" said Milord; then, annoyed at having been betrayed into a question,
he said he had supposed that we, like they,
were bound for St. Petersburg.

"Good-bye," said the secretary; "perhaps
we shall meet again!" He hung out of the
window waving his plaid travelling-cap as the
train carried them away.

II

An old barouche, two cream-colored ponies, and a patriarch with a long grey beard met us at the station. The patriarch's back was turned towards us (he was occupied with the skittish ponies), so *he* was none the wiser, only the station master saw us get out of the first-class carriage. Was he sufficiently impressed with our magnificence to make all that it had cost worth while?

Gertrude, handsome as ever, met us at the gate. Her face is firmer and finer than it was; she has kept her figure, is still tall and slender as a reed. There never was such a vibrant personality! At the gate, in her white morning dress, the breeze blowing her strong yellow hair, she looked like the wind spirit. She hardly gave us time to make ourselves fit to be seen before hurrying us to the *speisesaal* where her husband and all the In-laws were waiting to begin breakfast. The women are rather a frumpy lot (aristocratic frumpery). They looked like meek pea-hens beside their men, all dashing military fellows. I was glad Virginia had relented and worn her smart blue hopsack trimmed with black satin ribbons and wee gold buttons, the latest Paris fashion. Gertrude whispered on the way down that Virginia was "*zu schön*."

"Why," I whispered back, "did you make us wear our best clothes?"

"Oh, first impressions mean so much! Your trunks cannot be here for an hour."

"And *why* first class?"

"You will be treated better than if you had travelled second."

"*They* will never know."

"Trust them to find out!"

The chateau is a rambling old building of no particular style; the oldest part was built early in the seventeenth century, the newest a hundred years later. Gertrude says that house and people and everything about the estate are remote from anything else in the world — "Miles and miles away," she says, "years and years."

IN OLD POLAND

The *speisesaal* is an immense room with long windows, glass-handled doors, family portraits, and Berlin wool-worked chairs. The salon, even larger, is furnished in the style of 1830. The place reeks with war, always war! The two serious affairs of life here are war and potato brandy. In the hall is an old tattered French flag, found wrapped round the body of a French soldier, one of Poniatowski's men, a straggler from Napoleon's army in the retreat from Moscow. He was found in the wood near the house by one of the game-keepers, who took him in, nursed him, and when he died buried him. In the state bedroom is the bed in which Marshal Ney slept in 1807 on his way to join Napoleon before the battle of Eylau. A sabre carried at Sedan hangs over the mantel, on the antlers of a great deer shot by the man who owned the sabre; he was an uncle of the present incumbent. All the traditions of the family, you see, are of war, always of war. If the chateau is haunted, it must be by the ghosts of fighting men.

The estate is very large, ten thousand acres,

with two villages and a *brennerie* (distillery)
where some of the peasants are employed; the
others work in the potato fields. The day
after we arrived we had a good chance to see
the people; it was the master's birthday, no
work was done, and the old chateau was the
centre of hospitalities. In the morning there
was an audience for the serfs (they seemed
hardly better). The master received them on
the steps of the chateau. Gertrude stood beside him, all his family (her In-laws) grouped
around them. Each peasant as he came up
bowed low and kissed the hand of master and
mistress. The last to come up was a fine old
man with a face like an eagle, and very distinguished manners. As he stooped over the
master's hand, I recognized the patriarch who
had driven us from the station. My gorge rose
at the sight of this white-haired old man stoop-
ing to kiss the hand of the Herr lieutenant.
No man can like to kiss another man's hand, it's
out of nature. A woman's, especially when it
is milk-white like Gertrude's, is different; there
was some affection in that *hand kuss.*

"This is our good Peteroffski," said Gertrude. "You are to have the honor of driving our friends this afternoon, Peteroffski. Be sure and point out my favorite views."

"Peteroffski?" I said. "I know a young army officer of that name in my country — why, you look enough like him to be his father."

"I have a brother who went to America thirty years ago. I have lost sight of him. He married there, I heard of the birth of one son Solomon."

"I do not know the gentleman's first name, but I am sure he is your nephew — " I began.

"That will do, Peteroffski," interrupted the first In-law, a tall arrogant woman, "you may go now. To strangers, all people of one country look alike; it would have been impossible for the *gnadige Frau* to have known your brother's family."

The old man looked wistfully at me as he turned away. The In-law said something in an undertone.

"Don't you see," Gertrude explained, "it

would never do for one of our servants to imagine that any of my friends could be friends of his people — or that his nephew could possibly be an officer!"

"I do not see —"

"Take my word for it;" and the hand-kissing being over, Gertrude carried me off to the garden. I plotted a further talk with Peteroffski when he should be driving us. I reckoned without my host. Peteroffski was sent that afternoon to the horse fair at Dantzig to buy horses. We never saw him again.

The formal old garden is Gertrude's joy. The lilacs were still in bloom — fancy lilacs at the end of June. It has been a cruelly late spring, snow lying on the ground through April. Gertrude says the end of the winter is hard to bear. Snow begins in November. From Thanksgiving (she "keeps" it, poor darling, by always having roast turkey for dinner) till April she lives in a white marble world. She says she "cannot wait for spring," so she cuts boughs of willows and apple trees and puts them in vases of water in her warm sitting-room. The pussy-willows come out while there is snow outside; long before the orchard is in bloom spring and apple blossoms fill the pavilion.

"Is your Polish as good as your German?" I asked Gertrude. It seemed a simple question. She looked around to see if we were alone before answering.

"I understand it well and speak it fairly. I don't want *them* to know."

"Why?"

"Why, oh, why? You can't expect to understand everything at once. We try to suppress the Polish language; our peasants are supposed to talk German, none of *us* condescend to learn their language. I know a little Yiddish, too."

"Is there any truth in the stories of Jew baiting we see in the papers at home?"

"Before I came, there was trouble here. One Passover eve, the gardener's little son disappeared; he probably wandered through the woods and fell into the lake and was drowned.

Our peasants believed the Jews had spirited the child away and killed it to mix its blood with the unleavened bread of the Passover."

Life at the chateau is leisurely and luxurious. Nobody is in a hurry; that is the best luxury of all. Hedwig, Gertrude's jolly little German *mädchen*, brings our early breakfast to our room. She has flat braids of flaxen hair plaited in eight strands and wound round and round her head, china blue eyes, and red apple cheeks, pretty enough to give us an appetite for what she brings on her red and gold lacquered tray. Coffee, fresh butter, honey, and pumpernickel — like olives and caviare, a cultivated taste. We soon became converts to pumpernickel, a coarse black bread made of unbolted rye; it has a curious acid taste and is the mainstay of the peasants. Dinner is at seven, supper at ten. We have learned to eat five meals a day instead of three. It is the modern German theory to eat often and lightly. An American student in one of the big scientific laboratories at Stuttgart told me he had made the habit of taking

a snack every two hours, never eating a hearty
meal till night, when all his brain work was
done. There being no brain work for us here,
we get up appetites between meals by walks,
drives, rides, tennis, and croquet.

Our greatest festivity was a state dinner at
the nearest neighbor's, thirty miles away. We
went by train, carrying our evening dress,
dined, danced, supped, slept, breakfasted, and
came home the next day. The invitation was
returned in kind ; our hosts, and all the rest of
the party, becoming the guests of the chateau.
The ladies of the family supervised the prepa-
ration of the good things — they *were* good !
We are converts to the custom of always
serving " compote " with the roast, greengage
plums with roast chicken, cherry preserve with
ducks, etc.

The jam closet, linen-room, store-room, and
still-room are admirably arranged. These Prussian *grandes dames* seem more housewifely
than most women in the world to-day. It is
the trait in them I admired most.

One morning Gertrude appeared at lunch

evidently dressed for society. Everybody asked where she was going.

"To the forester's party," said Gertrude. There was a deal of laughter at this.

"Why, Gertrude, nobody is going. It was very foolish of the forester to attempt to give a reception," said the first In-law.

"Some one should have warned him," added another.

"We all like the forester. His bride is a pretty, charming young woman," said Gertrude, firmly, "and I am going to her reception."

"The forester is an excellent person," the first In-law admitted, "worthy of respect both as a government official and as a man. For their own sakes he and his young wife must be made to understand from the first that *here* professional standing and social position are two very different matters."

"Such people must be kept out of society; the bars are down, the rabble is rushing in," said the second In-law, a handsome cold-faced woman I had seen the day before on her knees binding up the wounded arm of the coachman's son.

" The obligation to preserve social tradition is sacred," said the last In-law, a callow youth in the uniform of a military academy ; " it is as bad to betray your caste as to betray your country or renounce your faith."

" Is n't fresh blood — are n't new ideas necessary to keep society from stagnating ? " I hazarded.

" That may be true of a commercial society," the first In-law cautiously admitted.

" They are vital to art, letters, science, the worlds of which 'society' is the parasite," I maintained.

" The American point of view is always so interesting, so original," said the first In-law, indulgently courteous to me as to a child.

They returned to the subject of the forester's party and threshed it out thoroughly. Each one, down to the last In-law, had a whack cither at Gertrude or at the forester. Virginia's eyes grew hard and bright as diamonds. I saw red. Gertrude's strong cool glance controlled us. The master of the house all this time was talking to his neighbor at table about ensilage. When the last In-law had had his say, and we were just rising from the table, the master said gallantly, —

"The carriage is ordered for you, my dear; take a warm cloak, the drive home through the forest will be cold."

The discussion was closed; we began to talk about the last book by Anatole France. They look to Paris for art, literature, and fashion as we did at home before we became more interested in the production of the native articles.

As we left the dining-room Virginia put her hand through Gertrude's arm, whispering in her ear, —

"I want to go with you to the party."

"No," said Gertrude, firmly, "I must go alone."

At dinner Gertrude had not yet returned; she was at supper, pale, tired, taciturn. She was afraid she would be asked about the reception. Her silence was handsomely covered by all the In-laws, who were uncommonly agree-

able.   We heard more good things said than at
all the other meals put together.   After supper
there was music in the big drawing-room ; the
master sang " The Two Grenadiers " in a mel-
low bass, the last In-law (that callow duckling
from the military academy) gave us " Adelaide."
He has a nice light tenor.   Then we all sang in
chorus the dear old German student songs, —
the very same Uncle Sam Ward brought home
from Heidelberg, part of the legacy of light and
song he left us.   " Was bringt der Postillion ? "
" Ach du lieber Augustin," " Es braust ein Ruf
wie Donnerhall."   We went to bed singing
" Eduard und Kunigunda" as we passed
through the long corridors of the rambling
old chateau to our quarters in the pavilion.

The night was chill.   Hedwig kindled a little
blaze in the high white porcelain tiled stove.
As we sat with our toes on the fender, hugging the fire, there came a tap at the door, and
Gertrude (in a very pretty violet kimono embroidered with wistaria) came in for a pow-wow.
The confidence, frozen by the fine manners of
the Prussian aristocrats, burst out in a flood,

as our great frozen river Kennebec, at the first spring warmth, melts and batters its dam of ice.

"It was too cruel," she cried. "The forester and his wife had made such splendid preparations. The house was gay with flowers and the pretty wedding silver. The young bride wore her bridal dress. A supper for fifty persons was laid out, and I was the only guest."

"What did it mean? Is there anything against him or her?"

"Nothing; everybody likes him, she is as sweet and pretty as a pink, but it has not been the custom here to notice the forester or his wife socially. He is a young man from another part of the country, and did not know this. They sent out cards to all the people within thirty miles — not one noticed the invitation or came."

"Brutes!" cried Virginia.

"No, not brutes, only fossils," said Gertrude, with tears in her blue eyes.

"He had brewed the punch himself; she had made a great white bridecake; ah! it

was too cruel." Gertrude had been wanting
to cry all day. Virginia and I sat down and
cried with her.

" Are you glad you went? Was it not
more awkward for them to have you see how
they had been treated ? " asked Virginia.

" I am glad *I* went," said Gertrude; " but
you see now why I would not take *you* to the
forester's party ! "

When Gertrude's hair was braided and tied
with lavender ribbons to match the wistaria,
we kissed all round and said good-night.

" Should you ever feel a desire to live in
the Pliocene Age," I said to Virginia when we
were alone, " marry a Prussian Junker officer."

" Gertrude's husband is a perfect prince ;
remember how he stood by her," Virginia
objected.

" He is a prince. But in the Pliocene Age,
under the feudal system, you marry the whole
family. If you must have a Prussian officer,
choose a healthy orphan, and if possible trans-
plant him to the U. S. A."

" You remember Gertrude's sister Mary ?

18   273

There was not much to choose between them when they were girls, was there ? "

" Granted ; next ? "

" I was thinking," said Virginia, "that I would rather live in Potztausand than at Tuxedo Park, like Mary. The cream-colored ponies are really more fun than an automobile. Looking out for the peasants who are earning your living must be more interesting than settlement work. If Mary gets tired of ' slumming,' fifty other women are ready to take her place. What Gertrude does *counts ;* she is like an Arctic discoverer cutting her way through floes of ice to the open polar sea."

" Yes, even in darkest Prussia the American woman 'counts' as you say. If man makes the opportunity, opportunity makes the woman."

" I wish," said Virginia, " that my brother Horace could learn to make a bow like that boy with the tenor voice."

It's just as well, don't you think, that our visit to Old Poland is at an end ? To-morrow we start for Southern Germany.